"I bet you're a barracuda in court. Telling people what to do is clearly your comfort zone. Whereas babies...not so much."

"It's that obvious?" Her cheeks flushed.

"Yup. When Ellie was crying earlier, you looked like you'd rather have a stroke than pick her up. Kids aren't that difficult. Despite what the diaper bag implies."

Vivian laughtoo. Too bad she a wide berth to. In h dency to argue and eally worked well

"I really don't know what I'm doing when it comes to babies," she said.

The soft admission made him forget all his reservations for a moment. She looked so beautiful right now, with her hair down and the questions in her face. He knew what it was like to doubt yourself, to wonder if you were doing the right thing. And maybe it was just the kindred spirit he saw in her, or maybe it was something more, but Nick shifted closer to Vivian.

"There," he said. "Was that so hard? Opening up. Letting your hair down." He toyed with a tendril that had escaped the pins. The silky strand slid across his fingers. "You really should do that more often."

"Maybe..." Her gaze met his and held. "Maybe I will."

THE STONE GAP INN...
Where Love Comes Home

Dear Reader,

I love, love, love Christmas. If I could start decorating in July, I would! So whenever I get to write a Christmas book, it's like living in the middle of the holiday. I play holiday music on my stereo, flip through past Christmas pictures—all in the name of "research," of course!

For *Their Unexpected Christmas Gift*, I knew I wanted to write a baby-on-the-doorstep story, but with a twist. And, I wanted to involve the Stone Gap Inn (because I love that place and wish it was real!) and bring in all the great Barlow family members, who pop in and out of the bed-and-breakfast.

But really, I wanted to write a story about finding home. Maybe it's because I'm getting a tiny bit older, but I think about the importance of home a lot more often now. Not the walls and the number of bedrooms in the house, but the actual home you build with people you love and who love you. I've lived in a lot of houses over the course of my life— small, big, run-down, grand—but the actual home I have now, with the dogs at my feet and Christmas favorites playing on the speaker, is hands down the best I've ever had. Not because of the location or the number of rooms, but because of the people within it (and the dogs are pretty awesome, too).

I hope you love this Christmas story about a baby who brings two strangers together, leading them to create a very special holiday for a very special little girl. And I hope that wherever your home is, it's cozy and filled with love and special memories.

Happy reading,

Shirley Jump

Their Unexpected Christmas Gift

———

Shirley Jump

HARLEQUIN® SPECIAL EDITION

Recycling programs
for this product may
not exist in your area.

ISBN-13: 978-1-335-57421-3

Their Unexpected Christmas Gift

Copyright © 2019 by Shirley Kawa-Jump, LLC

Printed in U.S.A.

New York Times and *USA TODAY* bestselling author **Shirley Jump** spends her days writing romance so she can avoid the towering stack of dirty dishes, eat copious amounts of chocolate and reward herself with trips to the mall. Visit her website at shirleyjump.com for author news and a book list, and follow her at Facebook.com/shirleyjump.author for giveaways and deep discussions about important things like chocolate and shoes.

Books by Shirley Jump

Harlequin Special Edition

The Stone Gap Inn

The Family He Didn't Expect

The Barlow Brothers

The Firefighter's Family Secret
The Tycoon's Proposal
The Instant Family Man
The Homecoming Queen Gets Her Man

Harlequin Romance

The Christmas Baby Surprise
The Matchmaker's Happy Ending
Mistletoe Kisses with the Billionaire
Return of the Last McKenna
How the Playboy Got Serious
One Day to Find a Husband
Family Christmas in Riverbend
The Princess Test

Visit the Author Profile page
at Harlequin.com for more titles.

To a Christmas I will never forget, with the man who makes every day better than the one before. Here's to many, many more!

Chapter One

Have a Holly Jolly Christmas!

Nick Jackson stood under the banner draped across the center of Main Street in Stone Gap, and debated sign sabotage. The entire town was in the process of getting decked out for Christmas. Elves—or rather, Department of Public Works employees in silly costumes festooned with bells—were on stepladders, draping garland over the street lamps. Shopkeepers were pasting images of fat Santas and fake snowflakes in their windows. Others were piping holiday tunes from their sound systems a full three days before the first day of December.

When Nick was young, he'd loved Christmas as much as any other kid, even though his parents hadn't been the traditional kind who woke up at dawn and had a pajamas-on-the-couch Christmas morning. They'd believed in dignified holidays, with practical gifts like suits and calculators. But for a kid of three, or five, or seven, the world still held magic and promise, and anything could happen. By the time he hit middle school, Nick had given up on miracles.

Until then, Nick had woken up at the crack of dawn every Christmas morning, then dragged his brothers Carson and Grady out of bed. He'd sat on the stool at the kitchen bar, fidgety and anxious and dreaming of finding something cool under the elegant, professionally decorated Christmas tree, like a race car or a skateboard. The three boys would wait through an interminable breakfast served by the cook, who shuffled around the kitchen and grumbled under her breath about being underpaid to make pancakes on a holiday morning.

Then their parents would wake, and there'd be a quiet, five-minute exchange of whatever sensible present had been chosen for the boys. Books, savings bonds, dress shoes. No Legos. No remote control cars. As holiday after holiday passed, and Nick began to realize there would never be one of those cozy family-by-the-fireplace scenes in the Jackson household, he'd told himself that when he was grown and out of his parents' house, his life would be different. He'd have the white picket fence, the Labrador and he'd flip pancakes for his kids himself every Sunday morning. He'd dreamed of that first Christmas, with all its perfection of a lazy morning by the tree. He'd even started filling in the image with his girlfriend, Ariel, and had been on the verge of proposing—up until she'd dumped him for his best friend.

The next day, Nick had hopped a plane to Stone Gap, North Carolina, to bury his grandmother and figure out what the hell to do next. After the funeral, he'd found out that Grandma Ida Mae had left Grady the house, and Nick and Carson each a nice sum of money. So he quit his job and stayed in Stone Gap, without a mustard seed of an idea of what he was going to do next. He had an inheritance to rely on once he decided, but that came with a few strings that Nick hadn't wanted to tackle yet.

After a month of scotch and self-pity. Della Barlow, owner and main chef at the Stone Gap Inn, got sick and left the kitchen understaffed. Nick had ended up taking her place temporarily, pinch hitting for Della and winning over the guests with his béchamel lasagna and lighter-than-air pancakes. By the end of that week, Nick had finally figured out what he wanted to do with his life at thirty.

He could have gone for another job in IT—he was certainly qualified for it, after several years working with his brother Carson at Tech Analysts. Somehow he'd slipped into a life of building computer security systems and analyzing hacker threats. Actually, it wasn't a somehow—Nick remembered the exact day he'd hung up his apron and toque and called Carson. The fight with his father, the confrontation when Richard Jackson found out his son had been lying about law school for over a semester.

The job with Carson was always supposed to be a

temporary measure, a stopgap, until Nick could save enough to go out on his own as a chef. One year had turned into two, had turned into four, and then he'd met Ariel, and leaving seemed like a bad idea. His cooking skills had gotten rusty, and he'd started to think he was too old to start over with a pipe dream. Until he'd found himself in the kitchen of the Stone Gap Inn. As the whisk turned wine and flour into a velvety sauce, his love of food returned. After she returned from being out sick, Della had offered him a job and Nick Jackson had had a purpose again, at least until he was done avoiding his life.

For now, he would be content to avoid the holiday season. He just wasn't quick enough.

"Hey, Nick! I forgot to say have a Merry Christmas!" Matty Gibson, the owner of Matty's Market, stepped out of the shop and gave Nick a wave. He was a tall guy, lean and lanky and with a balding dome hidden beneath a faded Atlanta Braves hat. Nick had heard that Matty had made it to the major leagues when he was only twenty, then tore his rotator cuff with a windup pitch that first spring training and had to leave before he played an actual pro game. He'd come back home to Stone Gap and eventually took over his father's grocery store downtown.

Nick worked up a smile of sorts. Could it at least be December before everyone started in on the holiday celebration? "Yeah, you too."

"So what are you making with all that stuff?" Matty nodded toward the paper sack. "I can't remember the last time anyone bought one of them jars of artichokes.

In fact, I don't think I've ever eaten an artichoke, jarred or otherwise. I only ordered them because Sadie down at the Clip 'n Curl said they're her favorite, and well, have you seen Sadie?"

Pretty much everyone in Stone Gap knew Matty had a crush on the owner of the hair salon. He'd asked her out twice, but she'd said no both times. As Matty told it, he had a bit of a reputation as a player, and Sadie wanted a steady man with a future. No amount of convincing had made Sadie change her mind so far about Matty's reliability as a boyfriend, but that didn't dissuade him one bit.

"I'm making a braised chicken with artichokes and cherry tomatoes," Nick said. "Nothing fancy."

Matty laughed. "Well, you use words like *braised*, and it sure sounds fancy. You have company coming or something?"

"Nope. Just me. There's no one staying at the inn tonight, so this is my dinner." He hadn't made any real friends in Stone Gap, just a lot of acquaintances. And that list included no one that he knew well enough to invite over to his room at the back of the inn. So tonight it was just him and the artichokes.

"Lot of work for one person." Matty shook his head. "Me, I usually just throw in a frozen pizza, kick my feet up and watch the game. These days, that's all I can do is watch the game." His gaze went to the distance, then he shook it off. "Anyway, you enjoy. See you around."

Nick said goodbye, then stuffed the bag of groceries in the cab of his truck. As he pulled away from downtown, he noticed the temperature had dropped since this morning, with winter taking as firm a hold as it could in North Carolina. It rarely got cold enough for snow, which was just fine with Nick. He'd had more than enough of below freezing temperatures when he lived up north. Plus, adding snow would just put the cap on *Holly Jolly* and he didn't need that.

Nick parked behind the inn, where a single door led into the kitchen, and his room, just to the left of the airy, sunny space. He supposed he could have texted and asked Grady, who had been the one to inherit the two-story, if he could live at their grandmother's now-empty house, but it had been easier to just stay here at the inn and settle into the small space that didn't hold any memories or connections to anyone else in his life. Bah humbug.

Okay, so yeah, maybe he sounded like Ebenezer Scrooge. All the more reason to just stick to his own company until at least January 1. Keep his head down, be alone and avoid human contact as much as possible.

Especially contact with his family. Grandma Ida Mae had left Nick a note in the package containing her will. A note he had read and set aside. What she wanted was too much to ask right now. Maybe ever.

An hour later, he'd stowed the groceries, done the few dishes from that morning and straightened the pillows in the front room. After a busy week for Thanksgiving, the renovated antebellum house was almost empty for the next two weeks, and then the Christmas rush began. Della had taken the opportunity to go away for a few days, leaving Mavis Beacham, her business partner, and Nick in charge of the inn.

As far as Nick knew, the only people currently staying at the inn were one elderly man who was visiting his daughter and grandchildren in town and two women who had shown up with a baby early yesterday. A blonde and a brunette, around his age. The brunette he'd only glimpsed a couple times, but she was one of those stunningly beautiful women whose presence lingered long after she left the room.

Nick hadn't talked to them, and they hadn't been social either, asking that their meals be left outside their door, and except for the occasional cry from the baby, the women had been pretty quiet. He made a mental note to ask the women if the baby needed any special foods. He assumed it was still drinking formula or whatever, but considering all that he knew about kids could be written on a grain of rice, Nick figured it didn't hurt to ask. There was some age when babies graduated to stuff like mashed bananas, right? Maybe the kid had already hit that milestone.

He had a couple hours until it was time to start his dinner. The women had asked for a late checkout today, and Mr. Grissom had already left to spend the afternoon and dinner with his family, which left Nick alone at the inn. Mavis would be in tomorrow morning, and they'd talk about the week's plan after breakfast. He liked that his life had settled into a routine of meals, cooking, cleaning, then rinse and repeat.

Nick stepped into the shower in the tiny bathroom attached to his room. The hot water eased the tension in his shoulders. By the time he turned off the tap, he was fit to be good company for himself. Just as he was stepping out of the shower, he heard a sound from the kitchen. It wasn't uncommon for guests to stop in and help themselves to a snack—free run of the kitchen was included in the price of the room—so the sound didn't worry him. He slipped on some jeans, threw on a T-shirt and thought he heard the front door of the inn shut with a soft snick, then the crunch of car tires on the crushed shell drive.

Nick took a few more minutes to comb his hair and tidy the bathroom before he ambled out to the kitchen. As he did, he heard a soft sound that began to grow louder by the second. It took him a moment to figure out that it was crying. And that the sound was coming from a small white basket sitting on the kitchen table, flanked by salt and pepper on one side and a cheery flower-patterned place mat on the other.

Correction—a white basket with a pink blanket and underneath the blanket…

A crying baby. An honest to God, miniature human. On the kitchen table. On a Sunday afternoon.

He hadn't seen the baby the women had checked in with yesterday—he had heard it cry only once in a while and had gotten a description secondhand from Mavis, who'd pronounced the baby the "cutest thing in the whole county," but he assumed it had to be that baby. It wasn't like babies rained down from the sky. At least, not in North Carolina.

But there was no one else in the kitchen. No one down the hall. No one at all.

He remembered the sound of the front door, the tires on the curved drive. He lingered in the kitchen, a few feet away, and waited. Surely they'd be right back.

But the door didn't open. The baby kept on crying. Not an ear-piercing wail, but more of a stunned, snarfling cry.

"Hey!" Nick called out to the emptiness. "Your baby is here!"

No answer. He grabbed the basket, holding it as delicately as a nuclear bomb, and dashed down the hall. He called up the stairs. "Hey, uh…ladies?" If Mavis had told him their names, he'd already forgotten them. "You forgot the kid."

Nick ran up the stairs, two at a time. His footsteps echoed in the empty house. He stopped at the Charlotte room, where he knew the women were staying, and knocked on the closed door. The door, which hadn't been shut entirely, swung open with a soft creak. "Um, just letting you know that your kid is downstairs. And seems…upset? Hungry? Wet? I don't know, but you should probably check on…um…her." Given the pink blanket, he figured "her" was probably a safe guess.

Silence. Nick peeked around the door, but saw nothing. Just the empty room. Which was pretty odd since he'd seen them check in with two sets of luggage.

It seemed pretty unlikely that they'd checked out and forgotten both a bag *and* a baby, no matter how much of a rush they were in. He returned downstairs, half expecting to see one of the women in the kitchen, apologizing and looking for the kid. But there was only the baby in the basket with him—crying louder now.

He bent down and tugged back the edge of the blanket. "Hey, there. What are you doing here?"

Even crying, she was a cute baby. Pink in her chubby cheeks, bright blue eyes and a flutter of blond curls on her head. Not that Nick had a lot of babies to compare this one to. In fact, the last time he'd been this close to a baby had been at his cousin Deanna's house three years ago on Easter, with his aunt Madge hovering over her "miracle" grandbaby like a helicopter. And even then, he hadn't gotten close enough to do much more than say congratulations, and back away before anyone got any ideas about making him do something like actually *hold* the baby.

"Stay here a sec," he said to the baby, who ignored him and kept on crying. Nick made a fast perimeter of the downstairs of the inn—living room, eat-in porch, dining room, den, then bathrooms one and two. No one else was inside the house. Just him and the baby.

"Where are your parents?" he asked the baby. No answer. Not that he really expected one. "Okay, then what am I supposed to do with you?"

Mavis's phone went straight to voice mail. Della didn't answer her phone either, but he didn't expect her to because she and her husband were on a cruise or something. The inn had a computer registry for guests—in Della's locked office. Mavis normally left the keys behind, but a quick glance at the hook in the pantry told him that she'd forgotten to do that today. So he moved on to his last resort. It took four rings before his mother picked up, her voice all breezy and cheery. The country club voice, as false as the Astroturf on the putting green of the back patio of the club. "Hello, Nicholas!"

"Mom, I...have a problem."

"I'm just heading into court. Can't it wait?" The friendly golf-course tones yielded to annoyance and impatience. Nick already regretted making the call, but it had seemed like the right choice. Find a baby on the kitchen table, call the woman who was biologically connected to you and therefore supposedly equipped for this kind of thing. Not that this was the kind of situation that had a guidebook.

He glanced down at the baby again. She'd stopped crying, thank goodness. But at some point she was going to start again, or need to be fed, or changed, or, well, raised into an adult. All things outside of Nick's capabilities. "Uh, no. This is kind of an urgent problem."

"Well, could you call your father or one of your brothers? Actually, your father is doing a deposition and I have this trial—"

"Mom, someone left a baby on my kitchen table and I don't know what to do with it." And his father wasn't talking to him, something his mother conveniently forgot whenever she wanted to pass the buck.

A long moment of silence. "Tell me this is a joke, Nicholas. What did you do? Did you impregnate some girl?"

He scowled. He should have known better. His mother lacked the maternal gene. The thought of her showing motherly concern for a stranger's baby was almost laughable, since the closest she could come to showing concern for her own son was to blame him for all of his problems. Some things never changed. She'd been the least maternal person he'd ever known, and had treated all three of her sons like mini-mes to their father, grooming the three of them to go into the family business of law. To achieve those goals, he and his brothers had been provided with nannies and maids and drivers and tutors, but when Nick had chosen a different path for himself, any hints of warmth or concern for him had vanished. What had made him think his mother would suddenly change in the course of a phone call? "I didn't do anything, Mom. Never mind. Sorry I interrupted you."

"Nick, if you truly have a baby there, call the fire department or something. Legally, you shouldn't touch that child because you could be sued if anything happens. The fire department will know what to do. There are safe haven laws—"

As always, Catherine Jackson went back to the comfort zone of the law. She was right, but that didn't mean he liked the option. "Yeah, thanks, Mom, I'll do that." Nick hung up, tucked his phone in his pocket, then paced his kitchen for a while. The baby stared up at him from her place in the basket, all wide-eyed and curious.

What was he going to do? He supposed he could call Colton Barlow down at the fire station and have him get the baby, the way his mother had instructed. But handing a baby off to someone he only sort of knew, especially at Christmas, seemed so wrong, so...cold.

Surely the whole thing had just been a mistake and the women would be back right away.

The baby's eyes began to water.

Oh God. She was going to start crying again. He poked around the blanket, careful not to disturb the infant, looking for a pacifier or a bottle—anything. All he saw in the basket was the baby and the blanket. The baby stared at him, ever closer to tears. "Hey, sorry. Just checking for a tag or something. Even Paddington Bear had one of those."

But the baby didn't. No supplies. No identification, at least not that he could see in his cursory look. No "if lost, return to" information. The baby started snarfling again and balled up her hands. *Don't cry, please don't cry.* "Kid, I don't have anything for you. I don't even know what to do with you."

The snarfle gave way to a hiccup, then a wail. She waved her hands and kicked her feet, dislodging the blanket, revealing pink socks over tiny feet and baby lambs marching across the baby's onesie.

"Oh, hell." He reached down and grabbed the baby. She was heavier than he'd expected, denser, and when he picked her up, she stopped crying and stared at him. "Well, hey there."

The baby blinked. Her eyes welled, and her cheeks reddened. Nick turned her to the right and did a sniff test. Nothing. Thank God. If there'd been a diaper situation, the kid would have been out of luck. She'd come with no instructions and no supplies. Maybe he should google baby care or something.

Then he saw the corner of a piece of paper, tucked

under the blanket at the bottom of the basket. With one hand, he fished it out and unfolded it. In neat, cursive script, the note said: "Please take care of Ellie as well as you took care of me. I know she'll have a good home with you. Love, Sammie."

Sammie. That was the name of one of the women, he remembered now. Who was the other one with her? Something with a *V*. Or maybe a *K*. Damn it. He couldn't remember.

"Ellie?" he said. The baby blinked at him. "Where's your mom or moms or aunt or whoever it was that brought you here?"

Ellie was holding her head up on her own, which was a good thing, he knew that much. It meant she wasn't brand-new, but also not old enough to make a peanut butter and jelly sandwich, so if he didn't figure something out soon, he was going to have to decide what—and how—to feed her.

"Kid, do you have teeth yet?"

The baby began to whimper. Nick brought her to his shoulder and began to rub her back in a circle. He'd seen someone do that in a movie once, and it seemed the kind of thing someone did to calm a baby down. Within seconds, it worked. The baby stopped crying, but then she did something worse.

She curled against Nick, fisted her hand in the collar of his shirt…and cooed.

"I'm not parent material, kid." Big blue eyes met his. Damn. He'd always been a sucker for blue eyes. "Don't get any ideas."

She kept on staring at him, nonplussed. As babies

went, she was pretty cool. And she smelled like straw-
berries and bananas, all sweet and innocent. Damn.
"What am I going to do with you?"

Just then, the front door opened and the brunette
who had checked in yesterday walked into the inn.
About damned time.

Nick kept the baby against his chest, grabbed the
basket with his other hand and hurried down the hall.
With each step, his aggravation with the woman grew.
It had been irresponsible as hell to leave a kid alone and
drive off, even if she had come back just a few minutes later. At the last second, he put the baby back in
the basket, then picked it up and carried it with him. If
this woman was the kind of mother who forgot her kid
on a kitchen table, maybe he shouldn't give her back
without asking a few questions. Or calling the cops.
"About time you came back, lady. You—"

"Why were *you* holding Ellie? Where's Sammie?"

Some of his anger derailed as soon as he was face-
to-face with the woman. She was just that beautiful in
her tailored navy suit and heels. She had her hair back
in a bun at her nape, her eyes hidden by sunglasses.
She had one fist on her hip, a circle of keys hanging
from her finger and an oversize boxy purse in the other
hand. For someone with a baby that he guesstimated
wasn't more than a couple months old, this woman
looked really, really great.

"Where is she? How am I supposed to know?"

Nick grabbed the basket and headed down the hall
to the kitchen and set the baby back on the table. "If
you're the kind of person who can't keep track of your

girlfriend or sister or whoever Sammie is, not to mention your kid, I'm not giving the baby back to you."

The woman ignored him. She barreled past Nick and crossed to the basket before Nick could react. "Ellie! Are you okay?" She pulled back the blanket, counting fingers and toes, acting all concerned.

Nick wasn't buying it. He yanked the basket up and out of the woman's reach. "What kind of mother are you, anyway? And who said you can even touch her? I should call the cops. I found her abandoned on the kitchen table in this basket. Anyone could have walked in and taken her, you know."

The woman put her hands out. "Thank you for taking care of her. Now, if I could just have the basket—"

Nick should have slammed the door in the woman's face or something. But he'd been all discombobulated by the baby on the table, and the sneaking suspicion that he was missing part of the story here. "I'm not letting you leave here with this baby. In fact, I'm calling the cops right now." He unlocked the cell and started pressing numbers. "I've seen *Dateline*, you know."

"I'm not the baby's mother—"

"All the more reason for me to call the cops, babynapper."

"I'm her aunt. My sister, Sammie, is the irresponsible one." She gave the baby a smile, but stayed a solid three feet away. "Ellie knows, doesn't she? I'm your auntie Viv."

Nick tucked his phone away. The two women were sisters, and the baby was this woman's niece. Made sense, but still didn't explain why the baby got left on the kitchen table. "Well, I want to see some ID."

The woman smiled. Holy hell, she had a beautiful smile. Wide and with a slightly higher lift on one side than the other. There was a tiny gap between her front teeth that Nick might have found endearing under other circumstances. "An ID? For Ellie? I don't think they hand out licenses to three-month-olds."

Three months old. Barely a person, which caused a roar of protectiveness in Nick. "Not for her. For you. Prove you're this kid's aunt."

"I can't. I mean, it's not like I run around with an ID saying I've got a niece. A niece I have only known about for twenty-four hours." She sighed. "I checked in yesterday, and you saw me then. Mavis checked my license and took my credit card, and…" Her voice trailed off. She opened her purse, took out her wallet and cursed. "Damn it, Sammie. She must have taken my AmEx when I was in the shower."

"You still have to pay for the room." The words felt way too weak as soon as they left his mouth. *This* was his biggest threat? After Sammie or Viv—a nice name for a woman like her, as if it was short for vivacious— had left the baby behind?

"Of course I will." She sighed, tucked her wallet away, then put out her hands again. "Give me the baby."

So maybe she was the aunt. It all seemed plausible. Her sister was clearly an irresponsible parent. What assurance did he have that this woman would be a better caretaker? Viv looked like a responsible human, but then again…didn't most people? Either way, she was still a stranger, and this kid wasn't old enough to talk, so Nick felt like he had to do some kind of due diligence. "Well, I can't let you leave with her, not until I know for sure that you're her aunt and that you're capable of taking decent care of her."

Viv crossed her arms over her chest. "I'm not going anywhere without Ellie."

They were caught in a standoff. And Nick wasn't going to budge. He looked down at the baby, at those big blue eyes that were so trusting and innocent, and knew he couldn't let the kid down. He'd found her, after all, and like a lost puppy, he was tasked with making sure wherever she went from here was safe and warm and good. The kid—*Ellie*, he told himself—had started to grow on him, damn it, and until he could figure out the right thing to do—

He did the only thing he could think of. "Do you want to stay for dinner?"

Chapter Two

Vivian stood in a stranger's kitchen, sitting beside Sammie's biggest screw-up yet. Not Ellie, of course. The baby was precious and innocent, and smelled like bananas and everything that made Vivian uncomfortable.

If there were two people who shouldn't be mothers, it was either of the Winthrop girls. Viv, whose entire life revolved around her career, and Sammie, her irresponsible younger sister who had dropped out of high school and run away more times than Viv could count. Sammie considered laws to be nothing more than a loose guideline to life, didn't believe in self-control or apparently birth control, and had left her three-month-old on the kitchen table of the inn when Vivian drove to a meeting in Durham that afternoon, then told Vivian by text.

Stupidity of the highest degree.

Vivian shouldn't be surprised. Sammie had never been what people would consider accountable. For anything. She wasn't Vivian's half sister—the daughter of boyfriend number seven or eight, who took Sammie to his mother's house after they broke up, then brought her back and dropped her off when Sammie was nine and "too much of a handful." From that first day when she'd found Sammie crying and alone, clutching a well-worn stuffed bear, Vivian had vowed to protect the girl.

The two of them had huddled in Vivian's bed, clutching each other and made a solemn vow—they would never leave each other. Never. And when they grew up, they would be good moms to their children and pick good dads.

Vivian had tried her best to keep those promises for as long as she could. There had been no kids for her— there hadn't even been any potential baby daddies— but she'd tried to stick close to Sammie, even as the two of them had ended up shuffled through the system like they were candy bars in a snack machine. She'd tried to steer Sammie toward college, or at least a trade, but Sammie had balked at any restrictions, and at eighteen, jetted off on her own, popping in once in a while to drop a bombshell—or, in this case, a practically brand-new baby—into Vivian's lap.

There were days when Vivian was pretty sure she was from another planet. Unlike her mother and Sammie, Vivian had a degree, a career, an apartment and a predictable, responsible life. She'd made a conscious decision not to settle down, not to have kids and to stick to her comfort zone—the law. When she was fourteen, she'd made that crazy promise with Sammie to be a good mother, but at thirty, Vivian knew better. She wasn't mother material. Not even close. So best to avoid all that hearth and home stuff and stick to her career. Except now here she was in a town she hadn't lived in for at least fifteen years, with a baby she didn't know, wondering why she kept cleaning up after Sammie.

This weekend was supposed to be all about bonding, about spending time with Sammie after more than a year since the last time they'd seen each other. Then Sammie had showed up at the inn with a baby in a basket, and said, "Surprise!" to Vivian, and everything had changed.

Vivian knew she should be resentful. But all she had to do was take one look at Ellie's precious sweet face, and she knew why she'd dropped everything and broken the land-speed record this afternoon to rush back to Stone Gap when Sammie texted: I can't handle it. I'm sorry. I left Ellie at the inn. Please take care of her. The little girl hadn't done anything wrong except be born to a mother who wasn't ready.

Sammie's drop and disappear act had created a massive problem for Vivian, though. She couldn't take care of a baby. Not just because she had neither a single mothering instinct nor any practical experience. Vivian had a demanding job. The law firm where she worked called her the "Results Queen" for good reason. There was a trial to prepare for and an apartment in Durham in the middle of renovations. Meanwhile, a baby required around the clock care. Vivian would have to hire a nanny and find a place that wasn't swarming with construction workers for the nanny and Ellie to stay, which would mean one more stranger in Ellie's short life.

"Want some coffee?"

She'd almost forgotten the man was there until he spoke. On an ordinary day, Viv would have noticed a man who looked like that. Tall, lean, dark-haired, with a smile that went on for days, and dark eyes the color of a good espresso. He'd been terribly protective of Ellie, which had frustrated Viv but also kind of endeared him to her. Even now, he hovered over her and the baby, clearly worried and not at all sure that Vivian could be trusted.

"I'd love some." She'd had an emergency meeting this afternoon that she'd tried to get out of, because she'd promised Sammie a weekend together. So she'd zipped up to make a quick appearance at the office, and just as quickly turned around again when the text from her sister came in, and all hell broke loose. Now Viv was going to have to come up with a plan for Ellie between here and Monday morning. "And thanks for the dinner invitation, but I really need to get back on the road."

"With the kid?"

"Well, I obviously can't leave her here," Vivian said as she got to her feet. Maybe she could get an Uber with a car seat, then come back for her own car later. Or call a friend to pick her up. Except she had no friends who weren't as career-driven as she was, and all of them lived at least an hour away. And right now, she was feeling pretty lost about what to do, a position Vivian didn't like being in. The man across from her, though, seemed cool and collected, and good with Ellie. "I… I don't even know your name." Why had she even said that? She didn't need to know his name. It had nothing to do with her getting back to Durham. She should be leaving, now.

"My name is Nick," he said. "Nick Jackson. There. Now I'm not a stranger."

The joke made her smile a tiny bit. Inside, her confidence shook like a sapling in the wind. How was she going to handle Ellie and work? And how would she know what to do if Ellie cried or needed something? Vivian knew her way around a courtroom, but not around an infant.

"I'm Vivian Winthrop. I'm a civil litigator, and Sammie is my irresponsible sort-of-sister who abandoned her baby here. I invited her to the inn for a weekend away and to spend some time with her. Sammie showed up with a baby I didn't know she even had, and then disappeared. Which is typical for her. She's been doing it since she and I were in foster care together."

"Foster care?" He arched a brow. Clearly, those words had put her back in the *reluctant to trust her* column.

"Sammie and I had a…difficult childhood with a mother who was…unreliable at best. It's just been the two of us most of our lives." Vivian fiddled with the handle on her coffee cup, avoiding Nick's gaze. That was about all she wanted to say about that. The less she thought about her childhood, the better. "Anyway, didn't you say something about dinner?"

He grinned. "So you're staying now? I take it you trust me now a little?"

"Well, I'm kind of hungry." She returned his smile and realized it had been a long time since she'd smiled. Her entire career was about being serious, a determined and stubborn bobcat in the courtroom and a moneymaker for the office. She'd risen quickly at Veritas Law based on that reputation, and had won several multimillion-dollar judgments and settlements against major corporations.

Her latest case, though, was more personal. A chance meeting with a man who was working nights as a janitor in the building revealed an injury that had nearly cost him everything. Jerry Higgins used to be a machine operator in a cannery, until a new piece of equipment with a faulty release switch had crushed his arm. The equipment manufacturer refused to cover Jerry's medical bills after the cannery's insurance company decided the equipment was at fault, not the cannery, which had left Jerry bankrupt. It was a step outside the usual lawsuits she worked, where one behemoth sued another, but it was also the first case she'd had in a long time that made her feel good.

Ever since she'd met Jerry, Vivian had slept, ate and lived that lawsuit. Even now, she could feel the need to get back to work. To finish that brief she needed to file, and schedule the next few depositions. Jerry, his wife and his children were counting on her to make it right.

Then she glanced over at Ellie, so innocent, so helpless in that wicker basket, and knew she couldn't go anywhere, at least not until she figured something out for her niece. Vivian might not be mommy material, but she was going to make sure Ellie was cared for. She'd need to call the office day care program and figure out a way to live amid the current chaos of her apartment before she tracked Sammie down. Right now, on top of her already unwieldy and bloated to-do list, "calling the day care" seemed like a Herculean task.

And besides, it was Sunday. She had only a few hours before the clock ticked over to Monday and her life got crazy again. But first, there was dinner with this man who seemed calm and strong, two things Viv wasn't feeling at all. Surely she had enough time to eat.

"I haven't had a home-cooked meal in…forever," Vivian said. "My apartment is under construction right now, not that I ever get in the kitchen and cook. So whatever you were making sounds good to me."

"Well then let me show you what you've been missing." Nick got to his feet and started pulling ingredients out of the refrigerator and a paper bag on the counter. Just then, Ellie started to cry, her fists rising above the blanket and waving in the air. The cries pierced the quiet of the kitchen, demanding, insistent.

Vivian rose and paced the small kitchen. Ellie kept on crying. "Uh, what's wrong with her?"

Nick looked as clueless as Vivian felt. "I don't know. She probably needs a diaper change or some food or something," he said. "Do you have any of that?"

Vivian gave him an are-you-kidding-me look. "Yeah.

I have all of that in my briefcase in the car. Of course I don't have any of that stuff. I'm not a mom, and Sammie didn't send me a grocery list when she texted me. She just said Ellie was here and she had left."

And Vivian had come running, as always. Bailing Sammie out. Again.

"Didn't she have one of those bag things?"

Vivian brightened. "She did have a shopping bag with some formula and a couple diapers. Let me see what she left behind." She ran upstairs and returned a moment later with the nearly empty bag. "One diaper and a mostly empty can of formula. I'm no expert, but that doesn't seem like enough." She sighed. Once again, Sammie had left her older sister to pick up the pieces.

"I know someone who might have some extra baby stuff." Nick picked up his cell and dialed a number. He tucked the phone against his shoulder, started chopping some onions and gestured to Vivian to pick up the baby, whose cry had turned into a wail. "Hey, Mac, it's Nick Jackson. I was wondering if you had some diapers and what do you call it…?"

Damned if Vivian knew. She stood beside the table, hesitant, while Ellie kept on crying. Pick up the baby? What if she did it wrong? What if that only made the crying—which was reaching police siren levels—worse?

Vivian tried tucking the blanket tighter—wasn't there something about burritoing a baby that soothed them?—and it didn't work. She tried sh-sh-shushing Ellie, and the cries only got louder and stronger.

Nick put a finger in one ear. "Yeah, formula. Bottles. Whatever a…" He turned and raised a questioning eyebrow in Vivian's direction.

"Three-month-old," she reminded him. That answer she had, but not much else. Ask her stats—born at three twenty in the morning, six pounds, three ounces, twenty inches long—and she could fill in the blanks. But quiz her on what age a baby started real food or how to change a diaper, and she'd fail in an instant.

The closest she'd gotten to Ellie before this minute was admiring her as Sammie held her. And that was as close as Vivian had intended to get. Until Sammie screwed up again.

"…a three-month-old baby. No, not mine, Mac. It's a long story." Nick paused a minute, then gave Vivian another pick-up-the-baby nod. "Thanks, buddy. I appreciate it." He hung up and tucked the phone in his pocket. "Mac will be by in a little while."

"Mac?" Ellie kept on crying. Vivian kept on standing there, hesitating.

What was wrong with her? If this had been a court case, she wouldn't have paused for a breath. But then, in a courtroom, she always knew exactly what to do. In those wooden rooms, Vivian was at home. While Nick's comfort zone was the kitchen, hers was in that space between the judge's bench and the plaintiff's table. She could deliver a one-hour closing summary to a jury of twelve strangers, but when it came to a single three-month-old…

Well, that was different.

"Della Barlow's son. Della's the co-owner of this

place, along with Mavis—you haven't met Della because she's on vacation right now." Nick walked past her, picked up Ellie and swung her against his chest, as if he did this every day. A second later, Ellie plopped her thumb in her mouth and her cries dropped to whimpers.

Vivian decided to act as if a strange man calming her niece was not at all unusual. Except a part of Viv felt like a failure. Weren't aunts supposed to be able to handle this kind of thing?

"The Barlows are a great family, in case you're worried. I've been the chef at the inn for about a month now, and I've met all of them." Nick had started swaying, a movement that seemed unconscious, and Ellie's eyes began to shut.

"Really?" Vivian felt a little jealous of her niece. Right now, Vivian was in that odd place between uncomfortable and unconfident, and could sure use someone else to soothe her own worries.

"You're so good with her," Vivian said.

"This is about the extent of my parenting abilities. So don't ask me to change a diaper or make a bottle." He chuckled.

If he asked her how to do either of those things, she wouldn't have an answer either. So she changed the subject. "So what are you making me for dinner, Chef Nick?"

"Braised chicken with cherry tomatoes and artichokes." He kept on swaying with Ellie.

"That sounds amazing. You made the eggs benedict we had this morning, right? Those were incredible.

Most of the time I'm eating popcorn or a sandwich grabbed on the run."

"That's no way to live. I think food is one of the greatest pleasures in life."

The way he said that made her a little weak in the knees. Which was insane. Vivian was a practical woman, not one of those who swooned or got caught up in romantic notions. No, that was Sammie, who was the believer in fairy tales and Prince Charmings, no matter how many times she got burned by guys who were more frog than prince—unemployed scam artists who wanted a free ride and a few bedroom benefits.

"Oh my God. Ellie's asleep," Vivian whispered. "How did you do that so easily?"

"I don't know. I just went with my instincts."

Maybe Vivian was lacking the necessary strands of DNA because she had no instincts for babies. Not so much as a blip of an idea when it came to making Ellie happy. Late last night, after Sammie and Ellie had fallen asleep, Vivian had stayed up ordering from some baby website, shipping everything from the "new mom gift suggestions" list she'd found there straight to Sammie's apartment. Baby outfits, blankets and a stroller that cost more than a small bus—because buying things was the only way Vivian could handle being an aunt.

Nick headed toward the kitchen table. Ellie stirred and let out a whimper. "Damn. I have to put her down to cook, but I'm afraid of waking her up."

"We can put the basket in the living room, so the

noise from cooking doesn't bother her. She'll sleep better there."

"I don't know if we should leave her alone, though." Nick kept on swaying. He glanced at the chicken on the counter, then the basket, then his gaze swiveled back to Vivian. Damn, he had nice eyes. And a nice smile. "I'm good with having her in the living room, but I think you should stay with her. Just in case."

That would give Vivian some time to check her phone, go over some emails and maybe kick off her shoes for a second. Then, after dinner, she could call a car seat–equipped Uber, get on the road with Ellie, and come up with a plan.

Because standing in this handsome man's kitchen, mesmerized by the way he calmed a baby to sleep, was sending her mind down an entirely wrong path.

Chapter Three

Nick was not a softie. Nope. Not one bit. And the sight of Vivian curled against a pillow, asleep, did not affect him one bit.

She was a beautiful woman, with dark hair that had partly escaped the tight, complicated knot at the base of her neck, big blue eyes that reminded him of the Atlantic Ocean a few miles away, and legs that went on for days. Her black heels sat on the floor, twin soldiers nestled against each other. The basket with the baby was on the carpet below where Vivian's head rested, Ellie snoring lightly in the dim room, and one of Vivian's hands resting protectively on the top of the basket.

If the circumstances had been different, this would have been his image of a perfect family. Mom asleep on the sofa, baby nearby, dinner simmering on the stove. But all of this was an illusion—a very temporary one at that. They weren't his family. They weren't his anything. After the meal, she'd be gone, and so would the baby.

He wasn't going to lie. The thought disappointed him a little. Maybe it was all those years of growing up in a house as sterile and emotionless as a roll of paper towels. Or maybe it was the holiday season nipping at his emotions, with the added bit of sentimentality being back in Stone Gap with his grandmother's house and all its memories a couple miles away. But a part of him wanted this moment to last.

Vivian stirred, blinked, then jerked upright. A detailed list and pile of neatly labeled folders slid from her lap. He could see a planner open and marked with a dozen checkmarks and color-coded tasks. Earlier, he'd heard her making calls, each one devoid of small talk and focused only on whatever document or information she was requesting. It was only when she'd fallen asleep that he'd seen the vulnerable, soft side of the driven attorney. "I'm sorry I fell asleep. I didn't mean—"

"It's no big deal. You had a hell of a day. All three of us did." The kid was still asleep, tiny and angelic in the white basket. As far as kids went, he kind of liked this one. She was easy to hold, easy to care for and easy to fall for. "I didn't want to wake you, but Mac's going to be here in a minute."

"Oh, yes, good." She got to her feet, smoothed her skirt, then pressed a hand to her hair.

"That bun thing is pretty much done." Nick grinned. "Beyond repair."

Vivian pulled out the pins that held the remains of the complicated-looking knot in place, sending her hair tumbling past her shoulders. Holy hell. Letting her hair down gave Vivian an unfettered quality.

Sexy. Tempting.

She twisted the hair, then tucked it back into the bun and pinned it in place again. Nick tried not to let his disappointment show.

This woman had efficiency down to a science. He suspected if he told her *you can't do that*, she'd say *hold my martini and watch me*. If she even let loose enough to drink a martini. She was as locked up—literally— as a summer cottage in the winter.

Vivian had said she was a corporate lawyer. He should have guessed that, from the severe suit and the practical heels and the references to a briefcase. If there was any kind of woman he didn't want in his life, it was a lawyer. Didn't matter what she looked like with her hair down.

His parents thought their law degrees gave them license to argue everything to death, put their careers ahead of their children time and time again. They had been there for their firm more than for anyone who'd ever needed them. Their marriage had been strained, and even at its best, they'd acted more like roommates than lovers. If that was life with a lawyer, he didn't want any part of it.

A soft knock sounded on the door. Nick hesitated for a second, still caught in the thoughts of Vivian with her hair down, then jerked himself back to the present and opened the door. Mac stepped inside, followed by Savannah. Their baby was nestled in a thing that looked like a backpack, affixed to Savannah's chest.

Mac and Savannah had been married for a couple of years, but they were the kind of couple that still held hands in public and gave each other secret smiles. Nick had to admit that their tendency for PDA had grown on him.

"Oh my. Is that her? I just want a peek at your cutie, Nick," Savannah said as she hurried past him and bee-lined to the kid.

He raised his hands and backed up. "Her name's Ellie. And she's not my baby."

Savannah had already reached Ellie. She smiled at the sleeping baby, then looked at Nick, then Vivian. "Your daughter is lovely."

"Oh, she's not mine either," Vivian said.

Mac chuckled. "Don't tell me you stole a baby, Nick."

"It's complicated," he said. Explaining it would sound crazy, for sure. Woman leaves baby on kitchen table, her irate sister shows up and stays for dinner. "Did you bring the stuff?"

God, it sounded like he was making a drug deal, not a baby supplies pickup.

"Yep." Mac swung a padded bag off his shoulder and left it on the hall table. Bright yellow giraffes and zebras cavorted on the outside of the vinyl bag. "Savannah and I got an extra diaper bag thing at her shower, so we filled it up with stuff you might need. Diapers, wipes, rash cream, formula, bottles—"

"Whoa, whoa. We're not invading Normandy here. I just have the kid for a few hours."

Savannah shot her husband a confused look. "Are you babysitting? Why don't you have any stuff?"

"It's a long story," Vivian and Nick said at the same time.

"Okaaaayyy," Mac said. "Well, we have a Mommy and Me thing to get to. And yes, I have become that dad." Mac glanced at his wife, then his baby, with such obvious love it almost hurt Nick to see the emotion. "Let us know if you need anything else."

Mac and Savannah said goodbye, then headed back out the door. Nick supposed he should have invited them to stay for dinner, but considering his dinner for one had already morphed into dinner for two, he wasn't sure he had enough food.

Though there was something to be said for having a full house. Nick had been in a decidedly deep self-pity slump ever since the thing with his ex-girlfriend, and having people here—not just inn guests that he dodged, but people he actually interacted with—was... nice. Nicer than he'd expected.

Maybe he should do what his grandmother asked and go see his father. Bring him that box that Ida Mae had left for her son. *It'll do you good to work things out with your father*, his grandmother had written. *And for him to realize what's important before it's too late.*

Nick hadn't even gone to the house to find the box, never mind picked up the phone. His father had made a fast, almost silent appearance at the funeral, exchanging maybe a dozen words with Nick's brothers, and none with Nick. Which was par for the course for the last ten years. Ever since the day he realized Nick had blown half his law school tuition on cooking school. He could still see his father walking away in disgust. *Why you would try to make a living out of something as foolish as cooking, I'll never know. You're a disappointment to me.*

He turned away from the door, and pushed the thoughts of the past from his head. It might have taken him ten years, but he was finally making a living at his dream job. Albeit, not the kind of money he'd made working with Carson, but not chump change, either. And he was happy.

Wasn't he?

"What is all this stuff?" Vivian peered inside the bag. With just her and the sleeping baby in the house, the inn had never felt so intimate before. "It's just a baby, right? Aren't they supposed to be easy?"

Nick chuckled. "I may not know anything about kids, but one thing I'm sure of, is that babies are complicated. Not as complicated as women but close."

Vivian parked a fist on her hip. "Women are complicated?"

He liked seeing this spark in her. This, Nick suspected, was the Vivian with her hair down. Unrestricted. Spontaneous. Intriguing. "Not all women."

"Then what kind of women are you talking about?" Vivian arched a brow. A half smile played at the edge of her lips.

Damn, she was beautiful. Interesting. He moved closer to her. She was wearing a perfume that lured him in—dark, deep, sexy. Like a garden after the sunset. Ellie went on sleeping, and the house went on being quiet and a world of just the two of them. "Women like you. With your practical heels and your suit and your bun."

"That's how I dress for work. What's wrong with it?"

"It's very…businesslike. Why are you working so hard to hide that you're beautiful?"

"You…" She swallowed. Her eyes widened, and the tough bravado dropped away. "You think I'm beautiful?"

"Oh come on, I can't be the first man to say that to you." Surely a woman like her had dozens of men lined up and eager for a chance to spend time with her. She was smart, confident and gorgeous. A trifecta.

"I… I don't date much." For the first time since he'd met her, Vivian looked embarrassed, unsure. "Nor do the men I work with ever say anything like that. Probably because I'm winning more cases than them, but still."

He laughed. "I bet you're a barracuda in court. I saw the battle strategy you had on the legal pad back there. Clearly, that's your comfort zone."

"It's that obvious?" Her cheeks flushed.

"Yep. When Ellie was crying earlier, you looked like you'd rather have a stroke than pick her up."

Vivian laughed. Damn, she had a nice laugh, too. Too bad she worked in the one field he gave a wide berth to. In his experience, lawyers had a tendency to argue and control, two things that never really worked well with Nick.

"I really don't know what I'm doing when it comes to babies," she said.

The soft admission made him forget all his reservations for a moment. She looked so beautiful right now, with her hair once again escaping the restraints of the pins, and the questions in her face. He knew what it was like to doubt yourself, to wonder if you were doing the right thing. And maybe it was just the kindred spirit he saw in her, or maybe it was something more, but Nick shifted closer to Vivian. "There," he said. "Was that so hard?"

"Was what so hard?"

"Opening up. Letting that hyperconfident facade drop." He smiled at her. "You really should do that more often."

"Maybe…" Her gaze met his and held. "Maybe I will."

Nick leaned closer, almost close enough to touch… and then Viv leaned in the rest of the way, bringing their lips together. Slow, easy, sweet, his lips meeting hers with a gentle pressure that begged her to let him in, let him know her. His hand reached up to cup the back of her head, to capture the stray brown locks that had escaped the bun. He kissed her, tenderly, leisurely—

And Viv started to cry.

Chapter Four

Vivian never betrayed weakness. Doing that meant certain death in the courtroom. She prided herself on keeping her emotions on a tight leash. It was part of what made her a formidable opponent. But the second she and Nick kissed it was like a dam had burst, and the tears that rarely showed in her eyes began falling.

This man—a total stranger—had seen a part of her that no one ever saw. The unsure, hesitant, out of her element Vivian, who had to ask for help. And despite that, he'd called her beautiful and been drawn to her enough for them to kiss.

She broke away from Nick and took several steps back. He was still six feet of tall, dark, handsome and tempting as hell. She swiped at her eyes, and tried to still her hammering heart with a deep breath. *What is wrong with me?*

There was nothing wrong with the kiss—that had been phenomenal. Tender, slow and easy, as if she was a dessert he wanted to savor. The scent of the food he'd been cooking—buttery and as warm and comforting as an early-fall day—lingered in the space between them. She had the most insane urge to put her head on his chest.

"I'm sorry," she said, the words giving her a moment to center herself, bring her heart and mind back to the world of common sense. A world where she didn't feel completely overwhelmed by a three-month-old and a dark-haired man with espresso eyes who called her beautiful. "I don't normally cry."

"I'm the one who should be apologizing. I thought..." He shook his head and managed to look both embarrassed and contrite at the same time. "Argh. I'm sorry."

"No, no, it's not that. I didn't cry because we kissed. I cried because..." *Because you saw a side of me I never let anyone see. Because you reminded me of what I've put to the side time and time again in my life. Because for a brief second, I was caught in a different world.* She didn't say any of that out loud. Instead, she resorted to a half-truth. "I'm stressed. I just...for the first time in my life, I don't know what to do."

She sighed and dropped onto the sofa. Easier to do that than to look at Nick and wish he would kiss her again. Maybe she'd been working too much or maybe it had been the *you're beautiful*, or the fact that she was so far out of her comfort zone with Ellie it might as well be another planet, but right now, Vivian felt as vulnerable as a fawn in an open meadow. That was not a place she liked to be. The walls she had erected decades ago crumbled a little, and everything inside her was trying to shore them up again, but it was like bracing against a tidal wave with a piece of cardboard.

Ellie had woken and was staring up at Vivian with that "do something, Aunt Viv" look. What could Vivian do? She was in such deep water that she was sure she'd drown and screw this up. Ellie needed a mother, not an aunt who was more comfortable with a deposition than a diaper. "I have a new client who is depending on me to go after this shoddy equipment manufacturer. I need to prepare for a potential trial, which means hours and hours and late nights and weekends of work. My apartment is in the middle of a total renovation. I don't have room or time for a baby. But I don't want to hire a stranger to watch Ellie, because…" She shook her head. Where were all these tears coming from? What was wrong with her?

Nick sat beside her. "Because what?" he asked, his voice soft, gentle. And another chink in those walls opened.

"Because Sammie and I spent our lives with strangers and we swore that when we grew up, we would never do that to our kids." The words came out in a whisper, words that edged along the secrets Vivian had kept close to her heart all her life. The vulnerabilities she hid behind the suits and the heels and the attitude.

Her childhood had been spent moving from one house to another, as her mother got sober, fell off the wagon, got sober again, a hamster wheel of changes. Some foster homes had been great, others had bordered on nightmarish. There'd been people who had refused to feed her unless she finished an endless list of chores. Foster parents who believed a belt was the best means of communication. Families she loved and said goodbye to before she could spend more than a handful of weeks there, the happiness she'd had with them just a fleeting mirage. Living her life out of grocery sacks and someone's worn, discarded luggage. Long before the roller coaster of foster care began, Vivian had taken one look at Sammie, so thin and scared and frail, and vowed to be the one person her little sister could depend on, the one person who would never leave her. It had taken a lot of fighting with the system and the rules, but Viv had done her best to keep her promise, until she'd graduated high school and gone on to college. She'd made the mistake of thinking Sammie would be okay once she was out on her own. Viv had been wrong.

Maybe it was being in this town again, in the same place where Viv had learned to roller skate and where she'd found out she hated beets but loved pancakes for dinner on Thursday nights that had her emotions running high.

"Then don't do it. Don't hire a stranger."

She glanced at Nick. "What are you talking about? I have to do my job, and I can't just leave Ellie home alone with the cabinet installers. Yes, they're strangers, but there's a day care at the office. It's not like she's going to be alone."

"Stay here tonight. Let me help you."

Let me help you. Four words that Vivian had never

before admitted she needed to hear. She glanced at her niece, at the pile of baby things that could have been a pile of books written in Greek for all she knew about them, and then back at Nick. "What time is dinner?"

Nick had made a lot of meals in his lifetime. So many, he'd lost count a long time ago. There was something about being in the kitchen, measuring and stirring and tasting, that centered him. As soon as he started cooking the rest of the world dropped away. Every single time.

Until he'd invited Vivian to stay for dinner, in his space, at his table. She wasn't even in the kitchen right now—she'd kept the baby in the living room to feed the baby some formula—which meant Nick should have been able to concentrate on the artichoke and tomato sauce.

Instead, as the chicken cooked in the braising liquid of wine and broth, he found himself listening to the sounds of Vivian talking to the baby in the other room. Her soft voice, nearly a whisper, captivated him. His mind kept straying from the recipe—memorized because he had made the dish a thousand times—so much that he ended up searching the internet for the ingredients list and forgetting what he had just searched a minute later.

She distracted him. And that couldn't be a good thing.

"Smells good."

He damned near cut his thumb off when he swiveled at the sound of her voice. Vivian was standing in the doorway, with the baby back in the basket. When he'd peeked in earlier, he saw that she hadn't held Ellie to feed her; instead she'd sat beside the basket with the bottle. He vaguely knew that babies had to burp after they ate, but how to make that happen…he had no idea. And clearly neither did she. Given the amount of "yucks" he'd heard as she changed Ellie's diaper, she was clueless with that as he was, too. He got the feeling that Vivian was about as comfortable with a baby as she would be with a hand grenade. Not that he was much more of a parental figure, so he had no room to talk. "Thanks. It was one of my grandmother's recipes."

Yeah, all cool, no betraying the little hiccup in his chest just then.

Vivian came into the kitchen and gestured toward the maple table. "Mind if I work a little and watch you cook?"

"Sure." He rarely had company in the kitchen because when the inn was fully booked, both Della and Mavis were busy with the guests and general housekeeping. When the inn was empty, there was no one around to check in on him while he cooked. And the last time he'd had a beautiful woman in his kitchen—

Well, it had been a while.

His ex-girlfriend Ariel hadn't come to his place that often, and he hadn't offered to cook for her more than a handful of times. After a busy day at the office, it was easier just to stop at a restaurant, grab a bite, then go back to her place for a few hours. He rarely slept over, and Ariel had rarely invited him. Now that he thought about it, their relationship had seemed to be

more one of convenience than anything else. No fireworks, no surprises, nothing but moving from one expected step to the next.

Well, until he received the totally unexpected, blind-
siding news about Jason. But looking back now, after
the anger had dissipated, his strongest emotion was a
whole lot of relief that he hadn't created a messy, legal
mistake by marrying her. With his parents, he'd seen
firsthand what an unhappy marriage looked like—the
chill in every conversation, the tight lips, the great
pains to avoid physical contact. Not what Nick wanted
for his future at all.

Which reminded him yet again that lawyer Vivian wasn't someone for him to consider for anything
beyond dinner tonight. She'd already told him in no
uncertain terms that she placed a high priority on her
career. Like his parents, her job consumed her life.
*Hours and hours of work, weeks and weeks of prepa-
ration.* The kind of single-minded workaholic tendencies Nick steered clear of, especially when associated
with a law degree.

Vivian sat down at the table, with Ellie in her basket
on the seat beside her. As if to prove his thoughts true,
Vivian set the almost empty bottle on the table, then
pulled out her enormous black leather planner and her
laptop. For a long time, there was only the sound of her
fingers on the keyboard and the soft coos of the baby.

After a while, Vivian sat back, stretched and
glanced over at Nick. "So, how's the chicken coming along?"

He shrugged. "Since I'm making it for two after

buying ingredients for one, I added some fresh linguini I made yesterday." He scooped a ladleful of starchy pasta water out of the pot, then stirred it into the artichoke sauce, which began to thicken, velvety and rich.

"You make your own pasta? I can barely boil water."

He picked up the pasta pot and crossed to the sink to drain it, then set the cooked pasta aside. "It's not that hard. It's almost…therapeutic to make pasta and bread. All that kneading is very zen."

Now it was her turn to laugh. "If there's one thing I could use, it's a little zen."

She did seem very uptight, as if she was held together with steel wires. That had been him, two months ago, when he was working with Carson and hating his job. "Growing up as the child of two lawyers, I know that lawyering is stressful. My parents operated on short fuses, still do. My brother Grady runs his own company, and my other brother and I used to provide tech support. None of us went into the family business, so my dad thinks we're all failures, except Grady because he has a lot of zeros in his paycheck. I thought my job was stressful, but Grady's was ten times worse. He was a working advertisement for avoiding that kind of thing."

He hadn't strung together that many words at one time in weeks. What was wrong with him? Pouring out his life story to a woman—a lawyer—who he barely knew? In his experience, nothing warm and fuzzy ever came out of a lawyer.

"And now you're cooking?"

The lilt on the end of her voice made it sound like

she thought he'd taken a step down the career ladder. And yes, he had in terms of salary and benefits, but his days were far less tense and most mornings, he rolled out of bed, his mind whirring with menus and ingredients and purpose instead of dread and tension. "It's where I'm happy. I think."

"You think?"

He used metal tongs to toss the pasta and sauce together. A quick taste, and then a dash of salt, and the meal was done. He grabbed two white plates out of the cabinet and set a fat twirl of pasta in the center, topped it with slices of chicken and a smattering of vegetables, then added sliced homemade bread on the side.

All to avoid answering that question of whether he was happy or not. The answer was complicated, and Nick didn't feel like explaining anything complicated right now.

"Dinner is served." He laid the plate before her with a little flourish, then handed her a rolled napkin with silverware tucked inside. "I can carry the baby upstairs, if you want to eat in your room again."

A part of him hoped she'd say yes, and leave him to his kitchen and his solitude. And another crazy part hoped she stayed and ate with him.

"Oh, well, I wasn't planning to eat in my room. I know I did before, but that was so I could visit with my sister, which really meant working a lot while she napped." Vivian frowned, then the placid face was back, erasing any emotion. "If it's okay, I'd like to stay here. I could use some company. I so rarely have any while I eat, and it's been a hell of a day."

Nick didn't eat with the guests. He'd grown to prefer his meals alone, or occasionally taken with Della or Mavis. He'd flick on the television in his room and let some mindless sitcom or movie he'd seen a hundred times fill the silence. That way he could mope and stew, and not have to answer any questions about why he was or wasn't happy. Or dwell on why he was still avoiding his grandmother's last request.

"Uh, yeah, sure." He grabbed the second plate and sat down across from Vivian. The baby had fallen back asleep, which was both good and bad. Good because sleeping baby equaled some peace and quiet, and bad, because sleeping baby meant there was no distraction between them.

Vivian dug in, swirling thick pieces of linguine onto her fork, along with saucy chunks of chicken and vegetables. As soon as she took the first bite, she smiled. "Oh my God, that's incredible," she said, the words coming out with a groan that sent Nick's mind down a path far from the kitchen.

"Uh, you have a little…" He reached toward her, then pulled back, with a reminder to himself that he wasn't supposed to be the guests' personal groomer. Even if said guest was beautiful and tasted like that first cup of coffee of the day. A little sweet, a little dark and a lot addicting.

Vivian wiped away the bit of sauce that had ended up on her chin. Without his help. Bummer.

"Sorry," she said. "I'm not usually such a mess when I eat. I'm just really hungry and this is really good."

"I'm glad you're enjoying it. I rarely have an audience for my food. Most of the time I'm in the kitchen cleaning up while the guests are eating."

In the space of time it took him to speak those few sentences, Vivian had wolfed down two more bites. "I haven't eaten since breakfast and didn't realize I was starving until now."

He chuckled. "You missed lunch? I would have gnawed off my arm by now."

She shrugged. "I very rarely eat during the day. When I do, it's a few quick bites at my desk. My days get so crazy busy that I forget."

He chuckled. "Honey, if you're forgetting to eat, then you're eating really boring food."

The *honey* hung in the air between them. It had slipped out of him, that Southern word that peppered almost every sentence down here in North Carolina and had invaded his own vocabulary now that he was back home. Vivian stared at him for a second, then dipped her head to take another bite. The memory of the feel of his lips against hers flitted through her mind, and she quickly changed the subject. "So, you're a chef instead of an IT guy. I get that. Sort of. More fulfilling and all that. But how did you end up here?"

"I grew up in Stone Gap, at least some of the time. My grandmother had a house in town, and my brothers and I were always pestering our parents to let us visit. We ended up here about once a month and if we were lucky, a week in the summer. Her house sits on Stone Gap Lake and was a thousand times better than the Mausoleum."

"The Mausoleum?"

"My parents have this monstrosity of a house with marble pillars and a lawn bigger than the state of Rhode Island, on a couple hundred acres up in Raleigh, where they work. The house was so damned big, we had to use an intercom system to find each other. My parents hated noise and so the house was almost always silent. Hence, the Mausoleum."

"We had very different childhoods," she said. "I don't think I lived anywhere quiet until I got a place on my own. Maybe that's why I still live alone."

Which implied no husband or live-in boyfriend. Why Nick cared, he couldn't say. Except that he couldn't forget kissing her or how much he wanted to do exactly that all over again. "I've lived with or near my brothers my entire life, until I came back to Stone Gap. Worked with them, ate dinner with them...we sort of became a tribe when we were younger, and that didn't change as adults."

"Until now." She speared a thick piece of chicken. "Why?"

"My life plans detoured." He took a sip of water and sat back, allowing the generous helping of food he'd just consumed to settle a bit. "I was dating this woman at work for a couple years. I planned to ask her to marry me, and to spend the week after Christmas in Jamaica to celebrate. Turns out she already had plans of her own—to dump me and go on vacation with my right-hand man and former best friend."

"Ouch."

"You can say that again. I was working so many hours, nose to the grindstone and all that, that I never even noticed the two of them had started hanging out more, finding reasons to talk to each other at work. The day after my would-be proposal turned into a breakup, my grandmother died. I came down here for the funeral and never went back."

"It's like a bad country song." A hint of a smile played on her lips. "Don't tell me you drive a pickup too?"

He laughed. "Actually, I do. But only because it's practical. Not because it carries my hunting rifles and Labrador."

A wider smile swung across her face. "This is good."

"You already said that. Twice."

"I meant the conversation. I forgot what it's like to talk to a normal person."

He wasn't sure whether to take that as a compliment or not. "Meaning someone other than a lawyer?"

She nodded. "All we do is argue."

So true. Nick had heard more hushed arguments between his parents in his house growing up than he'd heard conversations between them. On the upside, they were more interested in tearing into each other than yelling at their kids. On the downside, the reason seemed to be that they didn't much care about their kids at all. Not even enough to yell. His parents had rarely plugged in, hardly been a part of the boys' lives. Except for the time she'd worked, Vivian had surprised him by being far more engaged with him, dinner and the baby—more or less—than he'd expected. He'd held a firm no-dating-lawyers stance most of his life, but now, he considered easing that restriction.

Insane. She was only here for a couple days at the most. They weren't dating. This was just a shared meal in the kitchen. And there was a baby between them. Literally and figuratively.

"Tell that to my parents, will you?" Nick shook his head. "They never seemed to figure out how to talk to any of us boys, or each other, for that matter. Of course, we were also major disappointments because not a single one of us went into the law."

Nick almost had, being the one who'd tried the hardest to please his impossible-to-please parents. He'd lasted a little over a month in law school. One torturous, hellacious month of reading about tortes and case histories and evidentiary procedures before he bailed and lied to his parents for the next six months.

"I bet the guests at the Stone Gap Inn are really glad you didn't go into law. I know I am." She polished off her last bite, leaving the plate almost as clean as it had been when it came out of the dishwasher. "Is everything you make this delicious?"

He shrugged. "I think so. I mean, I just cook what I like to eat." That's how he'd always approached food— by instinct. He had the culinary degree, but he also regularly made it up as he went along. He seasoned by sense, rather than by exact measurements.

"Well, I'm eating whatever morsels are left in the pan and not being one bit shy about it." She rose.

At the same time, Nick got to his feet. "Let me," he said, putting his hand out for her plate. Their twin movements caused a quick, light collision. The plate wavered in her hands, almost toppled, before Nick caught it. Simultaneously, Vivian reached for his arm to steady herself.

Her lips parted in surprise and her eyes widened. "I… I'm sorry."

"It's my fault. Let me…" His voice trailed off as his mind went blank. It took a second for his hand to make the connection with his brain. "Uh, get you another helping."

"Thank you." Vivian dropped back into her chair, quickly, then whipped out her cell phone and busied herself with reading texts. The lightness disappeared from her features, replaced by the stern concentration of a workaholic.

If anything reminded Nick of what he didn't want, it was that.

Chapter Five

From the day she was born, Vivian Winthrop had spent every waking hour focused on excelling. When she was little, and living at home with a mother slipping deeper and deeper into an alcohol and pain-killer addiction, Vivian had worried over every single detail. Maybe if the beds were made and the house was clean and the dishes done, her mother wouldn't drink so often and yell so much. Maybe if she brought home perfect grades, her mother would notice and take her daughter to the park as a reward. Then maybe they could become a real family, like the ones she saw at school, with parents who scooped their kids into tight hugs in the parking lot after class let out. Maybe she could have a mom who marveled at the crafts and cookies from the Brownie meetings Vivian often had to miss because she had no way to get home afterward.

But the sparkling plates and hospital corners never earned a single word of praise. The A+ papers never got hung on the refrigerator. Every day, her mother retreated deeper and deeper into the shadows of her room and the solace she found in those wine bottles and the pills, until the state came in and decided Vivian and Sammie would be better off living with strangers. Every single time she and her sister were moved to another house, the cycle started all over again. *Let me be perfect*, she'd think, *and then maybe my mom will miss me enough to try harder, and she'll come get me.*

A psychologist would probably say she was trying to bring order to a chaotic life, but that quest for perfectionism had become an ingrained trait and made her a very successful lawyer. Vivian turned in every brief early, had the most organized office of any of the partners and dived into each case as if the fate of the world rested on the verdict. Meticulous, organized, perfect in every aspect of her life.

Until this weekend. Until Sammie up and ran away, leaving Ellie on the kitchen table. And leaving Vivian with the one thing she couldn't manage perfectly.

A baby.

And on top of that, the brief for the client she needed to write and file by Tuesday morning needed one more polish, the case law research was waiting on her review, and the emails she needed to return were multiplying like bunnies.

And Ellie was fussing and squirming, and on the verge of tears. She wasn't the only one.

"Come on, Ellie, please help me out. You know I suck at this," Vivian said to her niece as she tried to change diaper number two. "If you could just, say, not move for thirty seconds, maybe I can get this diaper on and then you'd be happy and I could work. Please?"

Ellie just twisted back and forth, her cries getting stronger by the second. She was much like her mother, all piss and vinegar, and anxious to see the world. Vivian thought babies this young slept all the time. Apparently, Ellie didn't get the memo.

Vivian slipped the new diaper back under the baby's butt for the fourth time, then taped one side in place and tried to quickly flick out and affix the other piece of tape. At the same time, Ellie moved, balling up her fists, crunching her legs to her stomach. The tape landed askew, and showed a gap between the diaper and Ellie's left leg. Vivian already knew—as did her pantsuit—what happened when the diaper wasn't firmly in place, so she unstuck the tape, tried again, darting past Ellie's complaining and twisting, and wham, fourth time was the close-enough charm.

"Phew. I need a vacation after that." Vivian dropped onto the bed and rolled Ellie toward her. She tried to give Ellie the rest of her bottle, but the baby just shook her head. She had her lips pressed together and the tears were starting again, dissolving into cries.

"Here, Ellie. Let's finish your supper." She nuzzled the bottle against Ellie's lips.

Again, no luck. Wasn't she supposed to be hungry?

Ellie hadn't finished the bottle earlier, and Vivian was pretty sure she was supposed to. Was Vivian feeding her wrong? Was there a wrong way to put a bottle in a baby's mouth?

"Ellie, come on, please." Again, Ellie refused and her cries yielded to screams. "Come on, honey. Take this, and we'll get your pj's on, then go to sleep." Vivian tried to say it all in the happy-mommy voice that Nick used. As soon as she said it, Vivian realized she should have saved herself some effort and put the borrowed baby pajamas on right after changing Ellie, instead of re-dressing her in today's pink onesie.

Ellie kept screaming, and as she did, her chubby fist waved, her fingers opening and closing around a hunk of Vivian's hair. Ellie pulled, and Vivian was sure she'd just earned a bald spot. "Ouch! Hey, honey, don't do that to Auntie Viv. Since you're not hungry, and I changed your diaper, you must be sleepy, right?"

The baby's blue eyes were wide open, without a hint of sleepiness. Vivian, on the other hand, felt like she could sleep for a week.

"Umm…let's go for a walk. Maybe that will calm you down." Vivian fastened her hair into a messy ponytail on top of her head, then picked up Ellie and paced the room. Holding the baby still felt weird and unnatural, and Vivian was pretty sure she was doing it wrong. When Sammie picked up Ellie, her daughter nestled into her neck. But when Vivian held her niece, Ellie remained stiff and separate.

Ellie's long, drawn-out wails were going to wake up the elderly man staying in the room down the hall, if they hadn't already. When Vivian booked the weekend away at the B and B, she'd been caught in some delusion about a drawn-out overnight party with her sister, the kind of late-night gabfest they'd had when they were young. Adding the surprise of Ellie into the mix had meant everything revolved around the baby. Which was okay, because Ellie was adorable—from a distance and to everyone else in the inn, it seemed—and Sammie seemed to be a good mother. But in the end, Viv had retreated to her comfort zone of working while Sammie took care of the baby.

Why Sammie had ever thought Vivian would make a better mother than her, she'd never know. Sammie had that natural connection—not to mention three months of experience. Sammie was the one who could intuit Ellie's every need. Whereas Vivian felt as lost as she had on her first day of law school. At least there, she'd had professors and books to consult. In this small room, she had only Ellie and some fumbled one-handed Google searches on her phone.

"How about this?" Vivian yanked the pacifier out of the diaper bag, pressed it to Ellie's lips, but again the baby squirmed and cried and refused to open her mouth. How terrible were Vivian's maternal instincts if she couldn't even get her niece to take a pacifier? Wasn't that basic stuff?

"What were you thinking, Sammie?" she said to the room, to the air, to all the miles between her and her irresponsible sister. Vivian sighed, tucked the pacifier into the pocket of her sweats, then grabbed the half-empty formula bottle and headed downstairs. Maybe in the kitchen, Ellie's cries would be muffled enough to not disturb the other guest.

Or Nick.

She'd been thinking about that man altogether too much when she should be thinking about work. Before, she could always keep work running in her mind while she did any other task. Maybe it was the quaint town or maybe it was the addition of the baby, or maybe, just maybe, it was that kiss she'd been unable to forget, but for the past few hours, Nick Jackson had lingered at the edge of her every thought.

A single light burned over the kitchen sink, casting a golden glow over the stove, the kitchen table, the white tile. Just a few hours ago, Vivian had been sitting at that same table, enjoying what might have been the best meal of her life, with one of the most handsome men she'd ever dined with. Nick had an easy comfortableness about him, in the way he moved and talked, and especially in the way he kissed.

Ellie buried her face in Vivian's shoulder and kept on crying. A reminder that Vivian would do well to focus on her niece and not on a man who was a temporary detour in a life that had been planned since she'd gone to college and decided the best way to avoid being disappointed by relationships was to not have them.

Vivian bounced Ellie in her arms, but the baby only got more upset, balling up her fists and waving them in her aunt's face. Vivian paced around the kitchen island, whispering *shh-shh* in Ellie's ear. She cried louder. Vivian offered the pacifier again; Ellie spit it back out. And cried more.

Vivian dropped onto one of the bar stools, clutched her niece to her chest and wondered if crying was contagious, because she was doing it now, too.

"Need some help?"

Nick was standing in the doorway at the other end of the kitchen, clad in a pair of flannel pajama pants and nothing else. His chest was bare, muscular and, even in the middle of her despair, Vivian noticed. "She won't stop crying," she said, swiping away her own tears before Nick got close enough to see them. "It took me seven hundred tries to get her diaper on right. Both times. I think I'm feeding her wrong, and I think she might starve, because she barely ate, and she isn't sleeping, and what if I'm screwing her up and—"

Nick crossed the room in three quick strides, and covered her hand with his. "Shh," he said, just as she had with Ellie a moment before. "She's three months old. It takes years to screw up a kid."

That made Vivian laugh a little. "True."

"Maybe it's just tough on Ellie to have all these changes in her life, and that's why she's so grumpy."

Vivian glanced down at her squirming, unhappy niece. She thought of her sister and herself, and how they'd acted out after yet another change, another home. They'd been much older than Ellie, but perhaps the feelings of disquiet, of frustration, were the same for babies. "You think so?"

"Babies like structure," Nick said. "They like schedules. It helps them learn that their world is predictable, and gives them a strong foundation."

Was this the same man who'd called her a babynapper earlier today? The same one who had seemed as clueless as she felt? "Where did you learn that?"

Nick shrugged. "I read a little tonight. I couldn't sleep, and I figured if I read some stuff about babies, maybe I could be more help to you. You know, if you wanted the help."

"That is—" she sniffled and tried not to show the wave of relief that filled her "—the sweetest thing anyone has ever done for me."

"Oh, honey, that's nothing."

There it was again, the word *honey*. It rolled off his tongue so easily, and melted her resolve to steer clear of this temporary man. It also made fresh tears well in her eyes. It had to be the hours of trying to be a mom to a child who wasn't hers, of struggling to succeed at something and failing so badly, or maybe just the holiday decorations all around town making her maudlin, but hearing that Nick had read up on baby care in his spare time just to help her made her cry even harder.

"Here, let me take her," he said, gently tugging Ellie out of her arms. "Looks like you might need the binkie more."

That made Vivian laugh again, and stopped the flow of tears. She swiped at her eyes and drew in a deep breath. It was a few seconds before she noticed that Ellie had stopped crying, too. "What did you do?"

"Nothing," Nick said. He was swaying left to right, as easy as a swing in a spring breeze, Ellie cradled in his arms. When he tried the bottle and she refused it, he set the bottle on the counter, hefted Ellie over one shoulder, and began to pat her back and rub it in circles at the same time. Ellie let out a loud, long burp, then settled into Nick's arm in contentment. When he tried the bottle again, she took it in with greedy slurps, and in minutes the bottle was drained.

Vivian stared. "You are like the baby whisperer."

"Seriously, it was all in this article for first-time moms that I found on the internet. When they don't want to eat in the middle of a feeding, sometimes they need to be burped. Or just calmed. So I tried both. I read some stuff because I knew nothing before that." Nick went back to that easy sway, and Ellie's eyes began to drift shut. "You know, I've been thinking..."

When he didn't finish, she prompted, "About what?"

He lowered his voice, nodding toward a sleepy Ellie. "Well, having a baby at the inn is kind of impractical. Because she's bound to cry, and guests are bound to complain. And you don't really have anything to take care of her besides this basket and the stuff Mac and Savannah brought over, which was really only for a temporary stay. You might think this is a crazy idea, but why don't you and Ellie come and stay at my grand-mother's house with me? My brothers aren't going to care, I'm sure. Della is returning tomorrow from her vacation, so I don't have to stay at the inn every night anymore. My grandmother's house is on the lake, and the only neighbor is like a hundred years old, so the kid can scream at a hundred decibels and no one is going to complain."

Stay at his house? That was insane. She barely knew him. But then again, any man who researched baby care on the internet for a child he wasn't even related to had to be from pretty good beans, as one of her favorite foster dads used to say.

"I talked to Mavis earlier tonight, and she said she has an old crib and a car seat we could borrow. Her daughter's youngest is like three or four now, so she doesn't need it."

Cribs. Car seats. All things Vivian hadn't even thought about after Sammie left. She had some of those things being delivered to a Sammie who wasn't there to sign for the boxes. Damn it. Her mind had been on work, and when it wasn't on work, it was on getting Ellie to stop crying. And wondering when the hell Sammie was coming back to live up to her responsibilities.

Yet another sign that she was failing at temporary motherhood. Heck, even a half-decent aunt would have thought of all the things a baby might need and not just thrown a credit card at the list and forgotten about it. While Vivian had been trying to research case precedence in the state of North Carolina, Nick, a total stranger to both of them, had been rounding up stuff for a nursery.

"Maybe I should just call someone to take care of Ellie," Vivian said. "I'm clearly not cut out for this motherhood stuff."

"Who are you going to call? You said Sammie isn't answering your calls. Your mom is no longer alive." He gave her a lopsided grin. "And I don't think the Ghostbusters handle this kind of thing."

Vivian ignored the joke. "Well, there's nanny services and maybe Sammie has a relative... She is the legal mother, after all. I don't think the authorities will even let me keep her."

"You know where the authorities will make Ellie stay until they find that relative, right?"

Foster care. The exact fate Vivian wouldn't want her niece to suffer. Yes, there were some great foster homes—she'd been in two that were pretty good, out of the seven she'd stayed at—but there were also some terrible ones, and no one could predict what number the dice would land on.

The Langstons had been one of those families who hit seven and eleven. The Stone Gap family had been patient and kind, even though Vivian and Sammie had been dropped off in the middle of the night, with barely a bag of belongings between them. An emergency placement, the social worker said, but from the second they walked into the Langstons, it had never felt like anything other than home.

Ruth Langston opened her door and her arms to the girls, drawing them close and telling them it would all be okay. They'd woken up to cheesy scrambled eggs in the morning and fallen asleep to the sound of birds outside their windows. In between there were games of catch in the yard with John, trips to the ice cream parlor with Ruth, and one all-day shopping trip in Raleigh that had outfitted both girls for the new school year. Every one of the sixty-two days she had spent in the Langstons' home had been magical.

Then their mother had stayed sober long enough for the judge to return the girls to her care. The day they'd left the Langstons behind had been one of the hardest days of Vivian's life.

What would Ruth and John do? Would they pawn Ellie off or would they take her into their home and give her the love she so desperately needed?

Ellie had fallen asleep on Nick's shoulder. Her chest rose and fell in slow, even breaths. "Maybe I should pay you to be her temporary parent," Vivian said, only half-joking.

Nick chuckled. "For one, this was a fluke, her falling asleep on me. For another, I have a job, and for a third, I'd make a terrible parent."

"You're doing better than me." Which was depressing to admit.

Nick had a point—how *was* she going to do this alone? The Langstons had been a team, dividing and conquering everything from laundry to bedtime. But Vivian was only one person, who had a trial looming over her, a workload she would have to ignore to take care of Ellie, not to mention an apartment unfit for setting up a baby in right now. Maybe she could make room for Ellie in the second bedroom where she'd set up a futon for herself, but between the noise and the dust of construction…

"Were you serious about inviting us to stay with you at your grandmother's house?" The question popped out of Vivian's mouth before she could think it through.

"Completely."

She narrowed her eyes. "Why would you do that?"

"The kid has kind of grown on me. And…you look like you could use the help."

In her experience, few people did anything without expecting something in return. Especially a stranger. So if he didn't want a favor out of her, why make the offer? "Is this some kind of knight in shining armor complex or something?"

"Is this some kind of 'I'm too tough to accept help when it's dropped in my life' complex or something?"

For some reason, the retort made her laugh. She liked Nick, liked him a lot. And his kiss...well, that had been one of the best kisses she'd ever had, until she'd ruined it by crying. "Okay, maybe you're right. But that would be imposing too much. I can't possibly ask you to do that for free."

He grinned. "Oh, didn't I tell you my going rate for babysitting?"

She did a quick calculation of her bank account. The renovations were costing her a fortune, but a private nanny wouldn't be cheap if she went that route instead, and Nick was bound to charge less. "Whatever it is, I'm sure we can work out something equitable—"

He put his hand on hers and she stopped talking. Simply stopped. Maybe because every time Nick looked directly at her or touched her, she stopped thinking.

"I don't need money." He held her gaze and didn't say anything for a moment, as if weighing his words before they left his mouth. "Until today, my plan was to spend the holidays alone. Avoid people as much as possible, do a good job of Grinching it. But now...that idea doesn't sound as good as it did this morning. So why don't you and Ellie stay with me, keep me company with no complications, and we all get what we want."

"That's all?" She gave him a side-eye. "Then what was that kiss about?"

"Weakness." He grinned. "You're a beautiful woman, and I was mesmerized."

You're a beautiful woman. He'd said it twice now. And the way he looked at her... Well, that was no reason to agree to this crazy idea. But then she thought about the weeks she had ahead of her, the insanity of preparing for trial. Ellie did seem to like Nick, and Vivian could probably do a lot of her work from home. And during the hours when she was gone, maybe it would be okay with Mavis and Della for Nick to have Ellie around the inn—although Viv was leery of how that would work out. She didn't know this Della and Mavis, and didn't even really know Nick.

"This is going to sound nuts, but I've never had a traditional Christmas." He shrugged. "If you stay with me, it gives me an excuse to hang some lights and make some eggnog and cookies and have the kind of holiday normal people have."

Vivian had been prepared to say no. To do what she always did and handle the entire Ellie crisis alone. But the scent of the braised chicken from earlier tonight still filled the air, and the idea of a real Christmas, one with lights and presents and a tree, sounded insane... but nice. Like what she and Sammie had had that summer at the Langstons when she was fourteen. A brief peek into a normal life. A family. "On one condition."

"What's that?"

"I get to pick the tree." Then she put out her hand and shook with Nick, and told herself she wasn't making the most insane decision of her life because she was feeling overly sentimental.

The next afternoon, Nick loaded his pickup truck with the borrowed crib, car seat, enough diapers to cover a family of quintuplets, a bright pink playpen, a giant tub of baby clothes, and an equally giant container of toys, bottles, bibs and a lot of other things he couldn't have named if you paid him. Vivian had run into work long enough to file the brief, then stopped in at a Walmart and filled a cart with supplies before coming back to help Nick. Mavis shooed him out the door as soon as he finished making a chicken casserole for lunch, and told him she had the place under control for the rest of the day. "We've only got two guests checking in tonight. Della and I can take care of things for a few days, just like we did before you came along. You haven't had so much as an afternoon off since you got here. So go, shoo, and spend time with your baby."

"It's not my baby, Mavis."

"I know that. But the baby doesn't know." Mavis's trademark broad smile spread across her dark caramel face, then her features sobered. "And, if I remember right, you also have one other thing to take care of while you're at that house."

That's what he got for having a late-night conversation with Mavis after the reading of his grandmother's will. The comfort she'd offered at the time wasn't worth the price of the ongoing guilt trip about not tending to Ida Mae's final wishes. "That can wait."

Mavis pursed her lips. She was a sturdy woman, with a large heart and big arms that tended to hug about everyone she met. "Well, y'all have a good time. And remember, don't come back until Friday. Della and I can handle things just fine."

Vivian came out to the porch just then, with Ellie in the basket. She crossed to the truck, opened the back door, then stared at the car seat. "Uh..."

Mavis laughed. "Sweetie, those things just look intimidating. Here, let me show you what to do." She reached in the basket and picked up Ellie. "Aren't you just the cutest thing? Next to my grandkids, of course. We're gonna put you in the car seat, and then you can go for a little ride, okay?"

A minute later, Mavis had buckled Ellie in, talking the whole time, alternating between high-pitched baby talk for Ellie and stern car seat usage instructions for the adults. Nick learned more than he'd imagined there was to know about the hidden car seat latches in his truck's backseat, crash force, proper buckling and backward-facing baby seats. By the time he and Vivian were in the truck and on their way, facts and figures swam in his head.

"Who knew there was that much to know about a seat?" Vivian said. "Or that they'd be that complicated to operate? I think it's easier to replace a carburetor than install a car seat."

"Your sister didn't own one?"

Vivian shook her head. "Sammie was unprepared

for Ellie, pretty much like she's been unprepared for everything in her life. When she arrived here for our weekend away, she was holding a baby I didn't even know she had. I don't even think the friend who dropped her off had a car seat in it. The least she could have done was be smart enough to travel in an Uber that had a car seat already installed."

"You can do that?"

"Apparently."

"Man, there's an app for everything these days." He took a left, leaving the Stone Gap Inn in the rearview mirror. It felt weird driving away from the place that had been home for the past few weeks.

He glanced across the front seat. The sun streaming through the windows danced off the waves in Vivian's hair. She had put the front part back with a barrette but left the rest down, and he had the most insane urge to reach out and touch her, to run his fingers through those tresses and draw her against his chest.

For a second, his mind imagined them as a family, heading home from a day at the lake or a trip to the store or whatever it was that normal families did. Then he shook off the feeling and concentrated on the road. They were not a family, and this whole arrangement was far from normal.

"So, changing out a carburetor. You have direct experience with that?" he asked.

She shrugged. "Foster father number five had an auto repair business. That foster mom had a lot of kids—I think there were six of us in a tiny little house—so he'd take some of us to work with him. I wasn't allowed to stand around useless, so I learned basic car mechanics."

He chuckled. "You surprise me. Uptight lawyer who can also change the oil and replace a spark plug."

"I'm not uptight. I'm…dedicated to my job. I have to be. People depend on me." Vivian buried her nose in her phone, which just solidified Nick's point, but he held back from saying so. As they drove, Vivian read emails, sent texts and made two phone calls, all during the short ride to Ida Mae's house. Work Vivian was completely different from barefoot in the kitchen in the middle of the night Vivian. The softness he'd seen last night disappeared, replaced by a harsher, more strident voice and rigid posture.

By the time they arrived, she had her laptop out and was back on the phone. When he parked, Vivian covered the mouthpiece. "Just give me a second. I need to finish this call."

"Sure." Nick unloaded the crib, playpen and baby supplies while Vivian stayed with Ellie in the truck. He dug the spare key out of the flowerpot, opened the windows to air out the house, lifted the blinds that had been closed for two months and set up the crib in the spare bedroom. Ida Mae had moved into a downstairs bedroom in the last few months of her life, leaving the upstairs rooms untouched, although as far as he could tell, she'd kept up with the dusting and general cleaning. Three bedrooms, one small enough to serve as the nursery for his father when he was born. The baby furniture was gone, but the pale blue paint had stayed, a perfect accompaniment to the white dresser, white twin bed and white borrowed crib.

After the crib was set up, Nick stepped back and took in the scene. The bright day outside cast dust motes into the air. He could almost hear his grandmother exclaiming about the visitors. About how good it was to have a baby in the house again. People sitting at her dining room table.

Ida Mae had provided the closest thing to a normal, loving home life that Nick and his brothers ever had. The big two-story house seemed deflated, empty, without her gregarious, giving personality. How his father, who was about as warm as a Popsicle, had come from someone so loving and homey, Nick never knew. Either way, he was certain his grandmother would have approved of him inviting Ellie and Vivian to stay. Grady hadn't minded. Nick had texted him a couple hours ago and asked if they could stay there. *Do what you want,* Grady had said, *I don't want the house.*

Grady had his own issues with the family to work out, while Nick had a few left untended himself. Nick could almost hear his grandmother's voice in his head. *Call your father. Work this out. Now that you're in the house, you have no excuse not to get that box.*

Damn that request. He supposed he could lie to the attorney who had handled the will and say he'd called his father, then the lawyer would cut the check for Nick's part of the inheritance. The idea tempted him, but the thought of one more lie didn't. Nick pulled out his cell and dialed the office number for his parents' firm. He debated calling his father's cell, but wasn't so sure Richard would answer.

The automated operator rattled off Richard's extension. Nick punched it in, took a deep breath and waited while the phone rang once, twice. "Richard Jackson."

The deep timbre of his father's voice surprised Nick. He'd expected voicemail. No, *hoped* for voice mail. "Dad, it's Nick."

Silence. "I'm in the middle of something. I'll call you back."

Nick already knew there'd be no return call. He'd been down that road before with his father. "Grandma left you something at the house. She wants me to give it to you."

"Just put it in the mail."

"Grandma said I have to do this in person." She'd mentioned that three times in her letter to Nick. "It's part of the terms of her inheritance."

Richard scoffed. "Leave it to my mother to put something stupid like that in her will. Listen, I'm not going to contest it. Just mail me the box, and we'll pretend we abided by her request." Before Nick could reply, his father added, "Is that all? I have work to do. I'm sure you have my address still."

Then the call ended. Nick stared at the black screen of his phone and cursed his grandmother's request. He loved Ida Mae, but what had she been thinking?

If his father wanted that box, he could come here. Nick was through doing Richard's bidding.

Nick went back out to the truck, to find Vivian still in the same place he left her. Working. Of course. Had he expected anything else? The sour mood brought about by the phone call with Richard deepened. He gestured toward the house. "I have the—"

Vivian held up a finger. "I want those files by the end of the day. Get a courier to bring them to me. Uh, the address?" She glanced at Nick.

"Thirty-two Lakefront Road," he said.

"Thirty-two Lakefront Road," she repeated. "In Stone Gap. I'll be in tomorrow morning to go over the new discovery."

She hung up and tucked the phone into her purse. "Sorry about that. We're in the middle of an important case, plus have another half dozen in various stages of development, and—" The phone rang again. She peeked at the screen and gave Nick an apologetic smile. "I have to get this. It's my co-counsel. Can you…?"

"Sure, sure," Nick said as if it didn't bother him at all that she was ignoring her flesh and blood for yet another phone call. Reason number 203 why he shouldn't kiss this woman again.

He walked around to the backseat to unbuckle Ellie. She squirmed against his chest when he lifted her out of the car seat. He grabbed the tiny blanket that had been on top of her legs in the truck and wrapped it around her, even though the walk from driveway to house was only a few seconds long. There was a decided nip in the air, a preview taste of the winter to come.

Once inside, he bumped up the heat a few degrees, glad that Grady had kept paying the utility bills, then set Ellie in the playpen with a couple of stuffed animals and large round plastic rings to play with. She lay on her back, taking more interest in her fingers than anything around her.

And Nick stood there, realizing that he had gone from helping-out babysitter to single parent in the space of a two-mile drive. If he'd known Vivian was going to be working this much, he would have gone along with the idea of hiring a nanny. Either way, this wasn't the holiday he had been envisioning when he proposed the two of them move in with him.

A feeling of dread chased up his spine. All his life, he'd avoided getting involved with workaholic women, because he had seen firsthand how that dedication to the job above everything else hurt a family. He'd seen how his own workaholic tendencies had caused his relationship with Ariel to crumble, and could only be grateful there had been no kids involved to be hurt by it. The endless hours he'd spent working with Carson, while good because he got to spend time with his brother, had almost completely precluded Nick from having a life, and kept him so busy he hadn't even noticed when his own began to fall apart.

No matter how beautiful or intriguing Vivian Winthrop was, he would do well to steer clear of falling for a woman who put work ahead of everything else.

Ten minutes later, Vivian finally came inside. "Gosh, it's cold outside. Thanks for taking care of all that stuff and getting it into the house. What do you need me to do?"

"It's all done." He scowled. "Ellie is happily playing in the big pink pen, and your bags are in the room upstairs, across from the nursery."

"You did it all? Wow. You work fast. I meant to help but—" Her phone rang again, and before she finished the sentence, she was already involved in another conversation. Vivian wandered off to the kitchen, pacing as she spoke.

Whatever was happening on the other end of the conversation didn't seem to be going well, which meant Vivian would be tied up for a while. Maybe he was wrong, and maybe her nose to the grindstone was a temporary byproduct of something going wrong in this particular lawsuit. He sure hoped so.

Nick did a quick assessment of the cabinets and freezer. The fridge had been emptied by a well-meaning neighbor after Ida Mae's death, but the freezer still held a quartered chicken. He did, however, find a bottle of wine in the cabinet. He set the chicken on the counter to defrost for dinner. He'd have to run to the market later for more supplies.

"What do you mean they filed a countersuit?" Vivian cursed under her breath. "They think Jerry was responsible? That's bull. I should have been there in court. Getting the judge to dismiss that would've been a slam dunk, Al, and you should have been able to handle it." She paced the ten feet from the stove to the back door. "No, I'll write the response tonight. Did you get the deposition yet? Never mind. I'll handle it myself." She ended the call and put the phone in her bag. She pulled out her laptop and turned to Nick. "I hate to ask but—"

Another phone call. Another work emergency. Of course. Red flags were waving in his face like a cape with a bull. "Go ahead, work. I'm good for a little while. I need to go to the grocery store at some point, and we need to get your car. We can do both later."

"Sure, sure, I'll be done by three." Vivian set up a temporary office at one end of the dining room table. Within an hour, it looked like a complete workplace, filled with files from her bag, notepads strewn with scribbled notes, and sheets she'd printed from Ida Mae's printer. Nick swore he barely heard her take a breath between phone calls.

As the clock ticked past three, he stood to the side of the room, holding Ellie as she drank her afternoon bottle, and Vivian kept on working despite her promise to be done by then. Transport all of this a few miles north and he could have been in the Mausoleum. Where everything outside the law ceased to exist to his parents, including their children.

"What have we gotten ourselves into?" he whispered to Ellie. She just blinked and kept eating.

Chapter Six

By Wednesday, they had all settled into a routine. Vivian got up at five and was on the road to the office by six, long before Nick and Ellie woke up. She texted him every day before she left the office at six thirty, and made any needed grocery runs on her way home. Meanwhile, Nick took care of Ellie, the house and made the meals. After dinner, more often than not, Vivian retreated to the dining room to work. If she got to bed before one in the morning, she considered it a good day. She knew she should help more with the household chores and Ellie, but Nick seemed to have it all under control, and she had a workload that seemed to grow by the minute.

Several times throughout the day, she called and texted Sammie. She'd received one *I'm okay, don't worry*, but no other replies. Sammie had dropped off the face of the earth. Vivian realized how little she knew about her sister—she had no idea where Sammie worked or who Sammie's friends were.

Maybe she hadn't been as good of a sister as she'd thought. That troubled her, and nosed at the insecurities Vivian did her best to bury every day.

She pulled into the driveway of Nick's grandmother's house on Wednesday night, and realized she hadn't been outside during daylight hours in days. She left before the sun rose, returned after the sun had set. The only time she'd spent outside had been going to and from her car in the parking lot. Vivian turned off the sedan and glanced up at the house.

Two stories tall with a wide front porch, his late grandmother's home was painted a pale gray with lilac shutters and white trim. Rosebushes sat beneath the windows, with a thick lawn rolling toward the driveway and sidewalk. Far in the background sat Stone Gap Lake, a deep, dark blue oasis ringed by a few year-round homes.

But it was the golden light framed by the living room windows that drew her attention. Inside the house, she could see Nick, holding Ellie. He'd captured one of her little hands between two fingers and was smiling down at her.

As Vivian stepped out of the car, she heard music. A country song, Thomas Rhett, maybe, coming from inside the house. She stood in the driveway in the cold air, clutching the box of papers she needed to go through tonight, ignoring the weight of the overstuffed bag on her shoulder and the pain of her heels after a long day, and watched Nick glide around the room with her niece in his arms.

And felt like a failure.

Nick made it look so easy. He had from the minute Ellie had dropped into his life. As far as she could tell, every time he picked Ellie up, she calmed down. Every time he changed her diaper, she looked up at him like he was the most adored human on the planet. And every time he held her, she placed her head on his chest and fisted his shirt in her palm, as if she never wanted to let go.

When Vivian picked up her niece, Ellie cried. When she changed Ellie's diaper, the baby squirmed and fussed and the tape went askew. When she held Ellie, her niece twisted away and pitched a fit.

Vivian glanced down at the box in her hands, the files and notes stuffed inside that needed to be looked over tonight. Maybe it was best if she just concentrated on her job. Jerry and his family were counting on her to make it right, to help them get back to normal lives. They needed her.

Ellie, clearly, did not.

Vivian turned, opened the rear door of her car and returned the box and her bag to the backseat. She dug out her keys and was about to open the driver's side door when Nick stepped onto the porch. He had Ellie wrapped in a blanket to keep out the cold. The country song floated in the air between them.

"Dinner's almost ready," he said.

"Actually... I'm not staying."

"You're leaving again already? Why? You just got here. If you want to hold Ellie for a minute—" he held her niece out to her, and as if on cue, Ellie began to scream and protest "—I can put the pasta in—"

"That's why I'm leaving, Nick. Because if I hold Ellie, she's going to scream. If I spend time with her, she's going to cry. And in the end, she's only going to want you anyway, so why should I even try?" She shook her head before her damned emotions got ahold of her. Nick had drawn Ellie back to his chest, and in an instant, the infant went back to being happy and content. Even the thought of being with her aunt upset Ellie. How could Vivian be any kind of parent to a kid who hated the sight of her? Nick was a thousand times better at this than she was. "I have a lot of work to do tonight—"

"You've had a lot of work to do every night, Vivian. And every morning. And all day."

"It's my job, Nick. That's what they pay me to do." It occurred to her that they sounded like a bickering married couple. When had that happened? When had they gone from strangers to friends to some sort of weird partners?

"Not to the exclusion of having a life, Vivian. If you ask me, you're just using the work as an excuse to avoid living. Your sister clearly isn't the only one who runs away." He turned on his heel and went back into the house.

Vivian stood there, fuming in the cold. How dare he tell her how to live her life? To imply she was missing out by being a workaholic? Or that she was running away? Okay, so maybe some of that was true, but as soon as this lawsuit was over...

She shut the car door, marched up the stairs and into the house, ready to tell Nick off. She stopped in the middle of the hallway. In the last few days, she'd come home, beelined to the kitchen for a quick bite to eat, then rushed to the dining room for a couple hours of work, then took the back staircase up to her room in the wee hours of the morning. She hadn't had a moment to pause and look at the rest of the house.

The living room she had been in on Monday, with the couch that was as comfortable as a slice of heaven, was in the process of being transformed. Evergreen garlands wove in and out of fat white pillar candles on the fireplace mantel, and beneath that, a fire burned, safely behind a wrought-iron grate she didn't remember seeing before. A ceramic miniature Christmas tree with hundreds of tiny lights sat on the end table, and the plain glass bowl on the coffee table was now overflowing with red ribbons and thick pine cones. A pillow-sized fat stuffed Santa sat on the sofa, against a thick afghan printed with a snowy mountain scene. The hallway rug beneath her feet had been switched out for a white-and-blue one imprinted with a holiday scene of children sledding down the long runner.

The words she'd planned to fling at Nick died in her throat. "When did you do all this?"

"Over the last couple of days. Whenever Ellie was napping, I'd go up to my grandmother's attic and unearth some more boxes. I had...something I was supposed to find up there, but then I came across the

Christmas decorations and figured it would be nice to put them up. So Ellie and I decorated."

Something he was supposed to find in his grandmother's attic? He didn't elaborate and she didn't ask. She did notice a lone box tucked away in the corner that was marked *Nick*, but didn't question it. This whole thing was temporary, a blip in her life, and getting more personal would be a mistake. "Ellie and you decorated?"

"Yep. I made her do all the heavy lifting while I watched." He grinned at the baby in his arms. "She's got quite the eye for mantel design."

"The room looks beautiful." She stowed her purse and keys on the end table, then stepped into the living room and did a slow spin. "It already looks like Christmas."

"Well, it will. We still need a tree. A real tree, not some plastic fake one that never sheds a needle." He waved toward the corner of the room. A few days ago, a small armchair had sat there. Now, the armchair had been moved to flank the sofa, leaving a blank space between the far left front windows and the wall. A stack of boxes labeled *Ornaments* was sitting on the floor beside the space. "I know this is a temporary situation with the three of us here, but I figured since it was Ellie's first Christmas, she might like the lights and stuff. She already thinks that Santa on the couch is a toy just for her."

Hard-nosed, dedicated, driven Vivian found herself tearing up for the third time in one week. Who was this man? And how did he happen to come into her life—and Ellie's life—exactly when they needed someone like him?

"So why don't you stay here tonight," Nick said, taking Vivian's hand and leading her farther into the living room, "and not work, and spend time with your niece and the man who made you fettuccini Alfredo for dinner?"

His hand felt nice on hers. Warm, safe, dependable. She curled her fingers over his. "You made fettuccini Alfredo? That's my favorite."

"I know. You mentioned it a couple days ago."

"And you remembered?" Damn it. Now her throat was thick, and her heart was full of some emotion she didn't recognize. She'd dated several men over the years, got sort of serious with a couple of them, but not a one could have named her favorite food, the flowers she loved best, or how she took her coffee in the morning. Nick paid attention to details—maybe that was part of the chef in him—and she'd already seen it pay dividends in the way he seemed to have an intuitive sense of what made Ellie happy.

And apparently, he also had a sense of what made Vivian choke up.

"Don't work tonight, Vivian," he said again, softer this time. "Let's eat and then go buy a tree, and decorate it tonight. I bet Ellie will love the lights."

She thought of the box in her car. Jerry sitting in the office conference room a few months ago and begged her to help them. The hours she and her team had put into this lawsuit already. She'd unearthed almost enough evidence of shoddy workmanship on the part of the manufacturer that she could go to them and hopefully negotiate a settlement and avoid a drawn-out lawsuit for that man and his family. Almost enough. A couple more days of work, and hopefully she'd have a solid argument for a hefty settlement.

"I have people depending on me," she said.

"You have a niece depending on you, too."

Vivian looked over at Nick. Ellie was nestled against his shoulder, her wide blue eyes fixed on his shirt. Her fist opened and closed over the soft cotton. "No, Nick. She's depending on you. And if you ask me, that's her best bet. Because I'm a lousy mother. And sister."

And I'm bailing just like Sammie did, bailing on Ellie, bailing on whatever this thing with Nick is.

Then she headed out of the house, got back in her car and drove to her apartment in Durham. At least there she wouldn't feel guilty staying up all night working and catching a nap on the futon in the spare room. And she wouldn't have to be reminded every time she turned around that she was letting down the one person she had sworn she'd never disappoint.

The next night, Nick tucked Ellie into bed, made sure her pink bunny footie pajamas were all snapped and that her room was warm enough. She had nodded off a few minutes earlier, about an hour before her regular bedtime, thanks to Nick skipping her usual late-afternoon nap and braving through the grumpiness that came after dinner. Nick headed back downstairs, set the table, then sat down to wait.

A week ago, he had scowled at the Christmas decorations going up around Stone Gap. He'd considered becoming a hermit until January 1, just to avoid all the cheery greetings and peppy Christmas carols. Then he'd found a baby on the kitchen table, and in the process of caring for her, he'd changed his mind about Christmas. Changed his mind about a lot of things, in fact.

Maybe he was more of a softie than he'd ever thought. Or maybe he didn't want to see another kid grow up in a Christmas void, like he had. Either way, he'd decided Ellie deserved a real Christmas—and he wasn't going to give it to her alone. Vivian had made a promise, and he intended to make sure she kept it.

Of course, all this was also a good way to avoid the request of his late grandmother. He'd found the box she'd mentioned in her letter, tucked in a corner of the attic. He'd done a cursory glance to find it filled with things from his father's childhood—baseball glove, stuffed bear, photo albums, a couple books. One of those leather-bound autograph books filled with signatures. *Build some common ground with him*, his grandmother had written. *You have more than you think.*

As far as Nick could see, he had no common ground with his father. He wasn't ready for another dismissive phone call, so the box sat in the corner of the living room, mocking his procrastination.

Ten minutes later, Vivian walked in. He heard the clatter of the giant bag she carried being set on the floor, the sigh that accompanied her kicking off her heels, then the soft patter of her bare feet down the hall. She stopped midstep when she saw him sitting at the dining room table. "Nick. You startled me. Sorry I'm so late."

"You're not late. You're coming home at the same time you've come home every day." He flicked out his wrist. "Just after seven."

She ignored the sarcasm in his tone. "Where's Ellie?"

"Asleep already."

"Already? Isn't that really early for her?"

"I'm surprised you know her bedtime." He sat back in the chair. The hallway clock ticked away the seconds.

Vivian scowled. "It's not like I haven't been here. Well, except for last night, but I had all this work to do—"

"What's the real story, Vivian?" Last night, when he'd confronted her and told her she was running away, she'd insisted he was wrong—just before she got in her car and, he presumed, went back to her Durham apartment for the night. He'd stayed up, staring at the ceiling above his bed, wondering why he had proposed this crazy idea of the two of them moving in together, and becoming a temporary family until Sammie returned. A few days at most, and then he had been sure Vivian's sister would show up. She'd left her baby behind, after all; surely she wouldn't do that on a permanent basis? But as day after day went by and Vivian's calls to Sammie went unanswered, Nick began to doubt the wisdom of agreeing to this arrangement. He'd had a different vision in his head than what it had become, that was for sure.

"Because you have avoided taking care of your niece since I met you," he said. "I offered to help you out, not become Mr. Mom. She's a great kid, really cute, and she's grown on me, but Ellie is not my daughter."

"She's not mine, either."

He got to his feet and crossed to Vivian. He paused a beat, holding her gaze before he spoke. "Well, she should be someone's, don't you think? She deserves a regular family."

"And why do you think I can offer that? I have no idea what a regular family is like." Vivian spun away and avoided Nick's gaze, just like she'd avoided this discussion for days. "I've got work to do."

"Not tonight." He got up and waved toward the seat across from him. "Tonight, we need to talk about this situation because it's got to change."

Vivian hesitated a moment longer, then dropped into her seat and took a sip of water from the glass on the table. "I can't believe Sammie left her daughter behind. I thought she loved Ellie."

"She does, if you ask me. 'Please take care of Ellie as well as you took care of me. I know she'll have a good home with you.'" He sat down, then slid the note that had been in the basket that first day across the table to Vivian. "Maybe Sammie left her with you *because* she loved her daughter, and because she remembered how you protected her when she was little, and thought you would make a better mom than the state, or some other stranger."

"I'm no good at it. I've seen how Ellie looks at you,

and how she falls asleep just like that for you." Vivian snapped her fingers. "Every time I try to pick her up or change her diaper or feed her, she cries and tries to get away. She hates me."

"You need to try more. Babies need consistency—"

"Thank you, Mr. Parenting Tips, for all your advice, but I don't need you to lecture me on raising my niece."

Her defensiveness was all barbs, a porcupine striking first to avoid an attack, but when she spoke, her eyes watered and her lips trembled, and he realized the capable, strong and smart Vivian was feeling completely unwanted and incompetent. Maybe it was all compounded by the fact that the world expected women to automatically know what to do with babies. Or maybe she truly was overwhelmed by the whole thing. He understood that—those first few hours with Ellie, he'd been convinced he was going to break her or something—but that didn't mean he was going to give Vivian a pass.

But it did mean he wasn't going to beat her up for struggling. If there was one thing that Nick understood, it was feeling like you were never going to measure up to some impossible standard.

He removed the foil covering the chicken parmigiana he'd made for dinner, then dished up a breaded cutlet and some sauce onto Vivian's plate. He topped it with freshly shredded Parmesan cheese. The time it took him to do that eased the tension in the room and gave Vivian a moment to collect herself. "So you mean to tell me that you can take on a multimillion-dollar company in court, but you're going to be bested by a kid who can't even hold a spoon?"

The joke eased the stress on Vivian's features, and she shot him a relieved smile. "Well, that's different. Clients don't need bottles, and multimillion-dollar companies don't need me to change their diapers." She settled her napkin in her lap. "In court, I know what I'm doing. When it comes to Ellie...I don't."

"Well, here's an idea," he said conversationally and easy as he dished up his own plate. "Why don't you take tomorrow off? Completely off. No work, no office, no phone calls. You can spend the time with Ellie—"

Vivian paused, her fork halfway to her mouth. "Alone?"

"Not completely. You'll have me, sort of. I have to go back to work tomorrow, but you and Ellie can come with me to the inn. You'll be in charge when I'm in the kitchen. That way you're not completely on your own, and I'm not missing that little munchkin, which I have to admit I never thought I'd say. Anyway, how's that sound?" He'd already talked to Della and Mavis, who hadn't hesitated to agree that he could bring Ellie to the inn. Both of them, he suspected, wanted to gush over and spoil the blue-eyed little girl. Nick couldn't blame them. Ellie was pretty cute. If he ever had kids of his own—

Well, that wasn't going to happen. But if he had, he would want one who looked like Ellie.

"Wait, you have to go back to work tomorrow?" Vivian said. "I thought we had until Friday."

"Today is Thursday. And in five short hours, it will be Friday."

She did the math, then shook her head. "Wow. The week flew by faster than I thought. I can't take the day off. We're in the middle of trial prep. If you're going back to work, then I'll have to find a nanny. I can't—"

"Try bonding with your niece?" He leaned closer. "She's your flesh and blood, not mine. And you act like she's got the plague."

"She's just not comfortable with me."

"You haven't given her much of a chance to learn to be. She needs a parent, Vivian. She needs someone who's going to plug in and be there for her for eighteen years, if necessary. That person isn't me. I'm a stopgap, not a father."

"I have work to do." She started to get to her feet.

He put a hand over hers and stopped her. He barely knew Vivian and Ellie, but he was damned if he'd let one more kid grow up with distant parents. Maybe all Vivian needed was a nudge in the right direction—and a jump into the deep end of parenting, like he'd had. "I can tell you firsthand that workaholic parents make for some pretty lonely kids who spend their birthdays alone, open Christmas presents alone, and spend all the time in between wondering what they did wrong to make their parents avoid them."

She bit her lip and sank back into the seat. "I get that. My mother was a 'holic' too. Just not a working one."

"Then don't do that to Ellie." *Or to me*, he wanted to add. But he'd already decided after last night that their relationship would be strictly about the baby. Nothing more. If anything proved Vivian's priorities, it was her going back to Durham last night. "Before Ellie got left on the kitchen table, I couldn't tell you the right end of a diaper or how to buckle a car seat. But I learned because that kid needed someone to."

"You're a natural, though." She waved at the dinner, then the decorations in the living room. "You're so domestic and homey, Nick, and I say that with envy. I wish I could be that way, but I'm just not. At all. My apartment was decorated by a woman I hired at the furniture store. And it shows. The entire space has this impersonal showroom feel to it, which is partly my fault because I'm barely there. I don't even own Christmas decorations or travel knickknacks or a set of dishes I inherited from my grandmother." She gestured at the plates and silverware on the table. "The only thing I can cook is spaghetti, and even then I overcook the pasta more often than not. I'm good at one thing, being a lawyer. I can't offer something to Ellie that I don't even understand myself, so how can I be her family when I don't have that foundation of a family, of a home? It's like I've lived on a different planet all my life, and now you're asking me to live on Earth. I'm no good at being a mother or being a housekeeper or even a—" her voice softened to a whisper "—good sister."

"You blame yourself for Sammie taking off."

It wasn't a question because he already knew the answer. He'd seen that guilt in Vivian's eyes from the second she realized Ellie had been left behind on purpose. "It's not your fault, Viv. Your sister made her own choices."

"And almost all of them have been bad, for years now, no matter what I did to try to help her sort herself out. I tried, Nick, I tried so hard to steer her onto the right path. But she dropped out of high school and ran off, and even after I set her up with a tutor to help her get her GED, she took off the day before the test. If she had passed that test, there was a place at a community college waiting for her, a college I would have paid for. I tried to give her a path to a life that was different than the one we grew up with. I swore to her, Nick, that I'd make sure our lives would be different. And now..."

"Your lives *are* different."

Vivian scoffed. "How? Ellie is living with strangers. Sammie is God knows where, doing God knows what, because she's not answering her phone, and all I can do is pray she isn't in jail or wrapped around a tree somewhere. I'm trying to juggle all of it, without anyone getting hurt in the process." She shook her head. "I failed her, Nick. I failed the one person I swore I wouldn't."

"You haven't failed anyone, Vivian." But she looked away and wouldn't meet his gaze, hearing the words but refusing to believe them.

Nick toyed with his fork, his gaze on the pale yellow tablecloth that had covered Ida Mae's dining room table for as long as he could remember. There were a few stains on it, from a splash of red wine, a dollop of spaghetti sauce, and the time that Nick had finger painted with a can of oil paint he found in the garage. Unlike the tablecloths at the Mausoleum, which were pressed and pristine, this one had memories imprinted in every crease. Ida Mae had been as proud of this blemished tablecloth as his mother was of the fourteenth century vase she bought at a Christie's auction. Ida Mae saw the wrinkles and marks as evidence that "the tablecloth had lived a good life," as she used to say.

And it had. Nick hadn't been here nearly enough, but as he looked down at the tablecloth and recalled the memories that included it, he realized he wanted to live a good life, too. He wanted to have the messes and the wear and tear and the memories. If he ever got married, he didn't want to spend more time in the office than he did with his family. Ida Mae had set an example that Nick intended to follow.

Even if it meant dealing with his father in person, as she had requested. Knowing his grandmother, she'd had a good reason behind the ask.

"My father would tell you I'm a failure too," he said. "In fact, he told me that of all his sons, he especially hoped I'd never have children because I was such a disappointment to him. He told me I would ruin the family name by breeding more laziness into the world."

Vivian gasped. "Your father said that to you? Why on earth?"

"Because I dropped out of law school. To him, that was an unforgivable failure. But I was on thin ice with him even before then—for most of my life, really. I've never been the super successful one, and my mother and my professors, would tell you that I'm a slow and stubborn learner, especially compared to my brothers, and especially when I'm studying something I don't like. I have to agree."

Vivian frowned. "I can understand what it means to pick things up slowly, but what do you mean you were a stubborn learner? Isn't stubborn a good thing when you're learning—to have that determination to stick with it?"

Nick chuckled. "For some people, maybe. But that's not how my stubbornness played out. In culinary school, one of the basic tests is to make a French omelet. They're different from regular omelets, softer in the middle, with a fluffy texture. They're one of those dishes that you can't walk away from, not for a second. It takes constant movement and attention and perfect timing to make a good French omelet."

"I don't know if I've ever had one. You'll have to make me one sometime."

That implied they'd have breakfast together. Something he had to admit that despite all his internal protests against involvement with Vivian, he would like very, very much, after a leisurely evening in bed. Because as much as he kept trying to resist this woman, the cold, hard-nosed, driven lawyer Vivian, another part of him kept falling for the barefoot, messy hair vulnerable Vivian from the other night. "I'd love to."

A flush filled her cheeks, then she dropped her gaze to her plate and took a bite. A moment extended between them before he cleared his throat and erased it. "Anyway, I didn't want to do it the same way the head chef did. I made up my own method. And time and time again, my omelet was subpar. The middle would be overcooked or the bottom too crispy. But I was sure I could come up with a better way, and prove my professor, and decades of other chefs, wrong."

"And did you?"

He scoffed. "Nope. But that didn't mean I gave up right away. I stubbornly persisted for way too long. Once I caved and began making an omelet the way I was taught to, though, mine turned out to be the best in the class. I had to fail before I could figure out how to be successful. I've done that all my life."

"That's just so…brave." She sipped her water. "I've never been that way. I've always taken the path of least resistance."

"I would say the opposite, Vivian. The childhood you went through—that's not something most kids survive, never mind thrive under. You went on to law school, and built a successful career. That's bravery. That's strength."

She lowered her gaze and focused on cutting a piece of chicken. "On paper, yes, but in my personal life… not so much."

"I think you are a very harsh self-critic." He covered her hand with his, and for a second, her blue eyes met his, and that barefoot, midnight Vivian flickered in her gaze, then disappeared just as quickly. She pulled her hand out of his and went back to her dinner.

"How did you end up in culinary school?"

A deft change of subject. He should be grateful. Hadn't he just resolved five minutes ago to be baby-business-only with Vivian? "The university where I went to law school also offered a culinary arts program. I went down to the dean's office and switched programs. One good thing about your father not paying attention to you is that it took him two semesters to realize what had happened."

"What did he do?"

"Cut me off financially. One hundred percent." He shrugged, as if the moment hadn't stung. "I started working after classes as a dishwasher and a busboy, and then I took out a loan for the rest to finish getting my degree. But the payments were too much for me to handle on a sous chef's salary, so I went to work for my brother in IT security. It was a job I hated every single minute I was there, but I got used to the steady paycheck and kept making excuses not to walk away. The truth was, I shouldn't have been there in the first place. My brothers are both megastars. Grady makes millions running his own company, and Carson just got promoted to VP. They were both at the top of their classes in school, and even though they didn't become lawyers, they have impressive business cards, you know? Me, I'm a law school dropout and now a chef at a tiny B and B in North Carolina. In many people's eyes, I'm a failure. But at least I'm a happy failure, and if you ask me, that's success."

She shook her head and laughed. "I've never heard success described as happy failure."

It wouldn't have been the way he would have described himself or his life just a few short days ago. But something about being around Ellie had restored his belief in himself. Maybe it was the whole new life thing, or maybe it was just realizing that he didn't have to be perfect, not with his omelets or his diapering skills, to bring the people around him joy. "You asked me that first day if I was happy."

"I remember. You said 'I think.'"

"At the time, I was still moping about the ex-girlfriend, and bah humbugging my way through the Christmas season. I'd been a hermit since I moved to Stone Gap, only coming out of my room to cook meals for the guests, and usually eating alone. Then you and Ellie dropped into my life—literally—and reminded me of what did make me happy."

"What is that?" Her eyes held a genuine question, as if she hoped he'd give her the answers she'd climbed the mountain to find.

"Family." He smoothed a hand across the tablecloth, erasing a wrinkle. When he lifted his hand, the wrinkle reappeared, as stubborn as the stains and history etched in every inch of Ida Mae's home. "This house and my grandmother were an incredibly important part of my family. My brothers and I would come here and be totally different people than we were in the Mausoleum. I think I'd forgotten all that until now.

"I came to Stone Gap a month ago, bitter and disillusioned. Which is pretty much how my life went when I lived with my parents. But here, in this town, at the inn with Della and Mavis, and in this house with that kid I swore I wouldn't even like, and the Christmas decorations on the table and you, I have to say I've got a family, sort of, and I like it."

The lightness disappeared from her features. Her blue eyes clouded, and a wall seemed to fill the space between them. Vivian pushed her plate away and got to her feet. "Family is the one thing I can't give you, Nick. So stop trying to make that happen."

Chapter Seven

Ellie was crying.

That was the first thing Vivian noticed the next morning. She was usually gone before Ellie woke up, and when Vivian rolled over to check the clock in her room, she realized it had been unplugged. Sunlight was just beginning to peek through the windows. Crap. That meant she was late for work. She still had the rest of those case studies to review and the research report to read. The worker she was representing had given her a number to work with—the amount that he felt he needed from the settlement to get his life back on track. But until she had all her ducks in a row, though, there wouldn't be much for ammunition in getting the manufacturer to agree to the number of zeros on the offer. It was a critical day. Heck, every day was critical.

Vivian sprung out of bed, tugged on her robe and hurried downstairs to grab her phone. In the nursery upstairs, Ellie kept on crying, the sound echoing through the silent house. Where the hell was Nick?

She headed for the counter, where her phone usually sat, attached to the charger at night. The space was empty, save for a sheet of paper.

Remember the whole "why don't you take a day off" idea? I called your office and said you were sick today. Al said he'll handle everything with the lawsuit, so don't worry about a thing. I loaded the car seat in your car and went to work. Bottle for Ellie is in the fridge. Take the day off. You need it. And Ellie needs to get to know her aunt. Nick

Clearly, he'd been serious about her taking the day off. That's what she got for leaving their conversation unfinished last night. All the fears, worries, inadequacies that their talk at dinner had unearthed were the kind of thing Vivian did her level best to avoid, and here was Nick Jackson, determined to make her face it all in broad daylight. Damn that man.

For the hundredth time, she questioned Sammie's thoughts in leaving Ellie here with Vivian, the least motherly person on the planet. She was so far out of her comfort zone with the baby, she might as well be in another stratosphere. Why couldn't Nick understand that?

Vivian stared at the sheet of paper, then spun toward the hall where she'd dumped her laptop bag last night. Upstairs, Ellie's cries had become full-on feed-me-and-change-me-this-instant wails. "Hang on, El," Vivian called up the stairs. "Let me just—"

Her bag wasn't there. Instead, another note, tacked to the wall.

> I knew you'd try to work one way or the other. Laptop and phone are at the inn. Breakfast is at eight. Come join us.
> Nick

Vivian was going to kill Nick when she saw him. He'd forced her into taking the day off, even though she'd told him she didn't have the time. Couldn't afford to take her eyes off the case. Now she was going to have to skip work, for at least another hour, until she could get to the inn and get her laptop and phone back.

Meanwhile, Ellie's cries had reached decibels normally reserved for rock concerts. Vivian stood there, trying to figure out which she should do first. Change her? Feed her? Both?

Maybe feed her while she changed her? Was that even possible?

Either way, it sounded like a good plan, and one that would hopefully ease the wailing coming from upstairs. She hurried back into the kitchen, pulled out the bottle that was filled and waiting in the fridge, and found a third note attached to the plastic.

> Warm this in the pan of water on the stove. Remember, you want it to be body temperature.

Shake the bottle after you warm the formula, to make sure it's all evenly warm, and test the temperature by shaking a few drops on your wrist. And yes, change Ellie while you're waiting for the bottle. Diapers are next to the crib. You can do it, Viv. Babies aren't as complicated as lawsuits, believe me.

There's a French omelet waiting for you at the inn. With bacon. And blueberry muffins.
Nick

What was this man, a mind reader? And damned if the omelet, bacon and muffins didn't sound amazing. Her stomach growled, and if she'd been three months old, she might have cried and demanded the breakfast be brought to her.

A whisper of confidence trickled into Vivian. Maybe this wasn't all that hard. Maybe she could change Ellie and feed her, and get the two of them in the car and over to the inn for breakfast. It was, after all, the only way to get that deliciousness in her stomach and herself on her way to work. *Babies aren't as complicated as lawsuits.*

Vivian sure hoped Nick was right and that his belief in her wasn't misguided. She did as he instructed, setting the bottle in the pan of water that she started to heat before heading back upstairs and into Ellie's room. "Hey, sweetie. It's your Auntie Viv. Let's get your diaper changed, okay?"

Ellie stopped crying long enough to give Vivian a dubious stare. That was a good start, she hoped. Vivian grabbed a diaper and the box of wipes from the small table beside the crib, then reached for her niece. Ellie squirmed a little, but mostly looked curious and bewildered by the change in her morning routine.

"We've got this, right? We can handle it." The words had a lot more confidence in them than she felt. That whisper from before disappeared the minute she held her niece, still at arm's length, as if Ellie might explode at any second. She didn't have that easy casualness with Ellie that Nick had. Not ever…or maybe just not yet?

Since when have you accepted failure? she asked herself. She'd survived the nightmares of foster care, graduated near the top of her class in high school, then put herself through college followed by law school and risen to the top at Veritas Law in record time.

"Nick's right," she said to Ellie. "If I can argue with a multimillion-dollar company in court, I should be able to handle changing a three-month-old's diaper. It's not rocket science, right?"

Except the last time she'd attempted this, she had failed miserably. Nick made it look so simple. Maybe she was overthinking it.

She laid Ellie on the twin bed, then unsnapped the bottom of her niece's lilac-printed pajamas. Ellie's legs kicked and moved, and it took a couple tries to find and unfasten all the snaps, but a moment later, Vivian had the pajamas off and the wet diaper removed. A quick swipe with a couple of wipes and a clean bottom awaited a new diaper. "Success. Whoo! Wait, El. Don't pee on me, okay? I have to get the new one on.

Just give me a second. I've done this a couple times before—okay, really badly—but I can do it right this time."

She tried to think back to how she'd seen Nick do it, because he was definitely more adept at the diaper thing than Vivian had been—a diapering job which ultimately had to be fixed by Nick, because her bad taping job had fallen apart later. To his credit, Nick hadn't laughed at Vivian's lame diapering. Rather, he'd given her a few tips in that patient, calm way of his.

Center the diaper under Ellie's bottom, he'd said as he redid Ellie's diaper. *Make sure the front and back are evenly aligned. Set the tape across that top band, and fasten it tight enough so there's no gap in the legs.*

"Okay. We've got this." She said it more to herself than to Ellie. Before Vivian could keep puzzling over it anymore, she slipped the diaper under her niece, flipped out the tape on the left and then on the right, then pulled the sides tight as she pressed the tape down and over the marching monkeys on the front. The diaper miraculously stayed in place. She checked the left leg, then the right leg, and there didn't seem to be any gaps. "Wait. Did I actually do this?"

Ellie wiggled her legs, squirming against Vivian's hand of caution on her niece's chest. The diaper stayed put.

"Well, what do you know. Maybe I can handle this after all." She redid the snaps on the pajamas—changing Ellie into clothes seemed a little much for her first solo day—then picked the baby up and settled her against one hip. Ellie moved a millimeter closer than the last time Vivian had held her. A start, at least. "Let's try a bottle. Okay? Sound good?"

Ellie started to cry again, which Vivian took for *I don't care, I'm hungry*, and together, they headed downstairs and into the kitchen. For the first time in a long time, Vivian felt a tiny bit of optimism that maybe, just maybe, she could be the aunt Ellie deserved.

Mavis propped her fists on her hips and stood beside Nick while he mixed plump dark blueberries into fresh muffin batter. There were only a couple guests staying at the inn, both of whom had asked for a late breakfast, which gave Nick a little more time to prep a buffet in the dining room. Muffins first, then some bacon, waffles and eggs.

"Where is that baby, and why haven't you met with your father yet?" Mavis said.

Nick chuckled. "Well, good morning to you, too, Mavis."

"I know you're just avoiding the conversation your grandma asked you for, Mr. Nick Jackson. But it's got to be had. If there's one thing you should have learned from losing that sweet Ida Mae, it's that life is as short as an unlucky cat's tail."

He spooned the glistening batter into a paper-lined muffin tin, careful not to mash the fresh blueberries. "An unlucky cat? I don't think I've heard that phrase before."

Mavis ignored his attempts to shift the direction of the conversation. She handed him the jar of raw sugar, and watched while he sprinkled the muffin tops, then put the pan in the hot stove. In the oven, the sugar would harden, creating a sweet, crunchy topping. "I know you have your reasons why you don't talk to your father—"

"He chose to stop talking to me. And when I told him about Ida Mae's request, he said to just mail the box." Nick started some bacon sizzling in a cast iron pan.

"—but that doesn't mean you shouldn't reach out again and keep trying. Your grandmother, God rest her soul, was the kind of woman who forgave everyone, and just wanted her family to be happy and peaceful."

"Family" had never been a word he'd associated with his parents. It was as if Nick's childhood had happened on two different planets—the Mausoleum and Grandma's. Maybe it was because his father was an only child, or maybe it was part of his father's disdain for the small town where he grew up, but the elder Jackson had differentiated himself from his parents and his past as much as possible.

Nick cracked a couple eggs into a big bowl, added some buttermilk, then whisked in the dry ingredients for waffle batter. Once that was done, he set it aside and went back to the bacon. "That's never going to happen."

"Why do you have to be the thunderstorm on the picnic? You never know what's possible until you try, Nick." She put the empty mixing bowl from the muffins in the sink and ran some hot water over it. "Now, where's my temporary grandbaby?"

"Hopefully on her way over here." He was pretty sure Vivian was going to kill him when she saw him. But he stood by his actions. Even though he'd only known her a short while, he knew she would have found a way to work if he hadn't absconded with her laptop and cell phone. And as long as she put her work first, last and always, she was never going to truly bond with Ellie.

As if conjured up by the conversation, the front door to the inn opened and Vivian strode in, one hand carrying the baby carrier part of the car seat, the other holding Mac and Savannah's borrowed diaper bag. Instead of the severe suits she usually wore, Vivian was clad in a pair of butter-soft worn jeans, and a T-shirt with an image of one shark watching another trying to eat a plump lawyer under the words You're Gonna Need a Bigger Plate.

Her hair was out of its usual professional chignon, and loose around her shoulders. Her face was bare of makeup, which only highlighted her wide blue eyes and dark lashes.

Mavis nudged him. "Don't burn the bacon, Romeo."

He jerked his attention back to the stove. Reminded himself to play it cool. This whole thing was temporary, a deal for the holidays. She was a lawyer who clearly put her career ahead of everything else. If anything said Big Mistake, those two things did.

"Your evil plan worked," Vivian said to him. "I managed to successfully change Ellie, and feed her. She's even quiet right now. And dare I say it…happy."

He grinned. "I wouldn't call it an evil plan. But I'm glad you had a good morning with her."

"There's my little munchkin!" Mavis crossed the room, tugged Ellie out of her baby carrier and held her tight, covering Ellie's cheeks with kisses. "Oh, how I miss these baby days. I hope my daughter has at least two more little ones. There's nothing more fun than being a grandma, even a temporary one." She nuzzled Ellie's chest, and the baby's hand curled around Mavis's thumb. "Let's go visit Della, shall we? She's probably bored silly, paying bills in the office. Let's bring her some sunshine."

After they left the room, Vivian stowed the baby carrier in a kitchen chair, then leaned against the counter beside the stove. She let out a long breath. "Okay, I'm here. Now, where are my phone and laptop?"

"If I tell you, are you going to use them?"

"Of course I am. I have a job to do."

"Then I'm not going to tell you." He flipped the bacon strips. They sizzled and spattered in the hot pan. "Besides, you haven't even had breakfast. It's never good to work on an empty stomach."

"Come on, Nick, don't be childish. Let me do my job."

He avoided looking at her, and kept tending the bacon. In the other room, he could hear Mavis and Della exclaiming over Ellie's tiny feet and hands. "When was the last time you took a day off?" he asked Vivian.

She blew a lock of hair out of her face. "Two years ago. No, three."

"And did you actually take a vacation?"

She toed at the tile floor. "I had the flu."

"But you take off weekends and holidays, right?" He said the last with sarcasm. He already knew that answer, because he knew Vivian's type. He'd lived in that house, had watched that life. Even had a taste of it himself when he went to work with Carson. That job had been a constant, mind-numbing, soul-crushing hamster wheel that never stopped rolling. Just when you met one deadline, six more popped up in its place. It left almost no room for a personal life or anything outside of the office.

"What does that matter?" Vivian said. "I'm single, and I live alone. What is there for me to rush home to? I don't have a cat or a goldfish or so much as a potted plant. No one cares if I work a hundred hours a week."

"I care."

"Why? You hardly know me."

He stepped away from the bacon and shifted closer to her. Without makeup, he could see the dusting of freckles across her nose. Adorable. He softened, ignoring the ache to touch her. "Because I have seen where that path gets you. My parents are very good attorneys. Very busy and very wealthy. And very, very miserable."

"That doesn't mean I'll be the same."

He cocked his head and studied her. The defiant tilt of her jaw, the steely resolve in her eyes. "How happy are you, Vivian?"

She turned away and poured a cup of coffee for herself, adding a generous serving of cream. "I'm happy enough."

"And what kind of life is that?"

Instead of answering, she walked away, clutching the mug in both hands as if she was cold. She paused by the small window on the back door. Beyond the glass lay a long expanse of lawn, green grass rolling down to Stone Gap Lake, a similar view to the one from his grandmother's house a couple miles away.

Nick pulled the muffins out of the oven and set them on a waiting rack to cool. He turned off the bacon, lifting the crispy strips out of the grease and onto a thick stack of paper towels. He ladled waffle batter into the hot waffle iron, and worked his way through preparing two before Vivian spoke again.

"I don't think I know what it's like to be happy," she said softly. "Because just when I would think I was, or that I had found a place where I could bloom, it was all ripped away from me. I guess I've learned to never count on anything or anyone other than myself. I can control me. How much I work, how much money I make, how many people I let into my world. But I'm not sure that equates to happiness."

"If you ask me, that's kind of sad. Understandable, given your childhood, but still sad." He set the pile of hot waffles aside and covered them to keep them warm. Then he put the omelet pan over the heat and added some butter. While that melted, he whisked three eggs with a little water and salt until the mixture was frothy and light.

"It's my life, Nick. I don't know any other way to be."

"Then why don't you take today, and the opportunity Sammie dropped into your life, and see where it gets you?"

"It's not that easy." She watched out the window a little while longer, then sighed and crossed to the stove, watching him cook.

Every muscle in his body was attuned to her presence. To the soft swell of her breasts under the T-shirt and the way the jeans hugged her hips and legs. Her perfume wafted between them, and tempted him to move closer.

The butter foamed in the pan, and Nick poured in the eggs. He gripped the pan handle with one hand while he stirred with a silicone spatula with the other, moving the pan and the eggs at the same time. The cooked eggs moved to the center and the uncooked part rushed to the open edges. Over and over he repeated that step until the eggs were almost completely cooked. Then he shut off the heat, smoothed the top of the eggs and folded the omelet into thirds. He added a tiny pat of butter under the omelet, then tipped the pan toward one of the blue-and-white stoneware plates. The omelet slipped easily from the pan and onto the plate, looking like a pale yellow pillow of eggs. The whole process took maybe two minutes.

"Wow. That's almost a work of art."

"Well, taste it and see if it lives up to its appearance." He added two slices of bacon and a warm blueberry muffin to the plate, then handed it to Vivian. "Do you want a waffle too?"

"If I eat all of that, I might explode. Wait…is that real maple syrup?"

"Yep."

Vivian groaned. Nick would have paid a million dollars to be the reason she made that sound when he touched her. "That sounds good. Save me one." She stared toward the table, then paused and glanced at him. "Aren't you eating?"

"I have to serve breakfast to the guests first. I'm doing a buffet with an omelet station in the dining room. I'll eat later."

"That's no fun." She sat down at the table, spread a napkin across her lap and picked up her fork.

"Ah, but all the fun for me is in watching other people eat my creations." And even though he knew the guests were waiting for their breakfast, he turned and watched Vivian take her first bite.

A smile spread across her face, and she closed her eyes for a moment. "Wow. That's amazing. Velvety and buttery and not at all like I expected."

"A good French omelet will make you forget all other omelets. Sort of like a good man." What was he saying? Where the hell had that come from? Was he volunteering for the job?

"I wouldn't know." Her cheeks flushed. "I mean about the omelets. My breakfast is normally a granola bar eaten on the run—or just a cup of coffee if I'm really in a rush. And if I do a business breakfast, I'm too busy working and talking to eat more than a couple bites of anything."

"That's no fun," he said, repeating her words. He

really needed to get back to work, but he was enjoying this rare moment of being alone with Vivian more than he wanted to admit. Mavis and Della were still cooing over the baby, their voices carrying down the hall from the office. He could hear the guests milling about the dining room. And still he stayed.

"I've always looked at food as a means to an end, you know?" Vivian said. She paused to eat the rest of her omelet, and let out a little moan of satisfaction at the end.

Damn. Nick was never going to be able to concentrate on cooking if she kept doing that. All he wanted to do was hear her make those sounds in his bedroom. "You, uh—" he cleared his throat, refocused his attention "—enjoyed your breakfast?"

She nodded. "Very much. I never realized what an experience a meal could be if I just slowed down and appreciated every bite."

She had finished the eggs and bacon, and was slathering butter on her muffin. If only to stop thinking about kissing her, Nick grabbed the pot of coffee, topped off Vivian's mug and set the creamer on the table. The waffles, muffins and bacon waited for him to bring them to the dining room. "I…should get back to work."

A soft smile curved across her face, and her blue eyes held his. "That's no fun."

He stepped away from the stove, his focus narrowing to only Vivian. Just as he moved to cross the kitchen toward her, Mavis marched into the kitchen with Ellie in her arms. An interruption both welcome and frustrating. In an instant, the sexual tension between Vivian and Nick evaporated.

"We have decided we are going to kidnap this little munchkin tonight!" Mavis exclaimed. "Because Della and I think you two need to go out and have a date."

"Oh, we're not..." Vivian looked at Nick. Her cheeks flushed, as if they'd been caught kissing by her father. "We aren't..."

Dating Vivian would be a huge mistake. He already knew where this path ended. He'd had a taste of it for the past week. His parents' relationship was bad enough, but at least they shared similar goals. Selfish goals that meant neglecting their kids, but shared goals all the same. He and Vivian didn't want the same things at all. He wanted a family. She wanted a career, to the exclusion of everything else. They'd never be happy together in the long run. If he was smart, he'd say thanks but no thanks to Mavis and get back to work.

Instead, he poured another ladle of waffle mix into the iron, then turned to Vivian and said, "We should."

"We should...?" The question trailed off, and a flicker of mischief lit her eyes, maybe started by the decadence of blowing off work and indulging in real maple syrup. "That would be a full day of playing hooky for me. I don't think I've ever done that."

He wondered what else Vivian had yet to do. And how he could figure into that. "Then let's do it. We can grab some dinner and then go pick out that Christmas tree. Together."

"I'd like that, Nick." The whispered words were almost buried under the beep of the waffle iron, but he heard them. And told himself that the warmth he felt from them was just the steam from the iron. It couldn't be anything more.

Chapter Eight

When Ellie napped, Vivian was finally able to work. She'd opted to hole up for the day in Della's office with her laptop, because being in that kitchen with Nick this morning had been way too tempting. Not just to eat ten more omelets, the entire stack of waffles and every last blueberry muffin, but to touch him, kiss him and find out why he'd agreed to that crazy plan of a date tonight. The initial plan of a full day of playing hooky had been replaced by a full day of working and an evening off. Anything else was too distracting and awoke a craving inside her she'd never known before.

An insane part of her was looking forward to the whole thing. She hadn't been on a date in over a year, and had never picked out a Christmas tree. The few holidays that she'd had when she was in foster care had been half-hearted at best, with overwhelmed temporary parents and houses full of kids. Every year, her mother had promised. *I'm gonna get you girls back, and we're gonna have the best Christmas you've ever seen. I'm just waiting on a paycheck*—or the courts or a man or whatever the excuse was that year—*and then I'm gonna get you and we'll be a family again.*

Even before foster care, there had been broken promises and empty dinner tables. Vivian stopped believing in her mother a lot sooner than she stopped believing in Santa Claus. There were no Christmas miracles, just a lot of empty promises.

But maybe this year she could create a little Christmas magic for Ellie. Her niece wouldn't remember it, but years down the road, Vivian could show her pictures, and tell her that for her first Christmas, there had been a tree and a Santa.

Vivian took a sip of lemonade—yet another homey touch from Della and Mavis—then got back to work on an email reply to the equipment manufacturer's legal team. They wanted to avoid the lengthy court trial and millions it would likely cost them by settling out of court. The settlement they offered, however, wasn't enough, not without an admission of guilt and a recall of all other similar machines in use in factories across the country. Vivian didn't just want justice—she wanted to protect anyone else from suffering as Jerry and his family had.

She glanced over at Ellie, who had just nodded off. The day with Ellie had gone smoother than Vivian expected, mostly because there were plenty of hands on deck whenever Ellie was awake. It hadn't been the trial by fire that Vivian had expected, thank God. Nick had popped into the office between shifts in the kitchen, but a guest who asked for a last-minute birthday cake kept him busy most of the day. Between chores around the inn, Mavis and Della hovered around the office, ready to offer advice when Vivian was feeding or changing her, and to pick up Ellie the second she let out so much as a squeak.

Vivian had researched the Stone Gap Inn before making the reservation for her and Sammie, so she'd known that the place would be comfortable and well-maintained, but the surprise—during her stay, and then during this unexpected day visiting the inn—was how big a role the owners played in making the inn such a wonderful place.

Della Barlow and Mavis Beacham welcomed every guest at the Stone Gap Inn with a Southern drawl, a warm hug and a friendly smile. Their gracious Southern hospitality matched the rooms at the inn, with their big, fluffy comforters and deep, floral-patterned armchairs. Wicker baskets overflowing with local goodies—jams, cookies, candles—waited in every guestroom for new arrivals. If there was ever a place that could be called a home away from home, it was the Stone Gap Inn.

Little wonder, then, that Ellie responded well to both the environment and the women fussing over her. All the attention wore Ellie out, and she napped without complaint, twice in the morning and once already this afternoon.

Della rapped lightly on the open door. "Care for some company with your lunch?"

Normally, Vivian would say no because she often worked while she nibbled. But today was technically a day off, as Al reminded her in a stern voice every time she called him, and Ellie was asleep in the playpen set up in the corner of the office, so it might be nice to have some girl time with one of the inn's owners. A few minutes of that wouldn't make a big difference in her workday. She could always make up the time after five.

Except there was that "date" with Nick tonight that she'd agreed to. Dinner alone, before Christmas tree shopping. A part of her kept getting distracted by the idea of being alone with Nick. Of the possibility of him kissing her again.

"Sure, come on in," Vivian said. She caught the scents of toasted bread and something fruity, and her stomach rumbled.

Vivian cleared a space at the desk for Della, then took her plate. "Thank you for bringing me this."

"Nick's in the kitchen, whipping up some buttercream frosting. He says baking is not his thing, but I tasted the cake batter and it was delicious. Who knew such a simple thing as a white cake with buttercream frosting could taste like heaven?" Della had a friendly face, eyes that seemed to dance every time she talked and deep red hair that spoke of a lively spark in her personality. She loved her boys, her husband and her town with a fierceness that Vivian envied.

"Just like the muffins this morning," Vivian replied.

"Nick is an incredible chef. He made something as simple as eggs, bacon and muffins into something that could rival any five-star restaurant. And this…" She glanced down at her plate. "Is this a panini?"

Della nodded. "Turkey and Swiss with homemade raspberry jam and watercress on rye bread. With a side of sweet potato fries and a cinnamon dipping sauce."

Vivian's mouth watered. The sandwich was perfectly toasted, glistening with warm butter. A dollop of raspberry jam slowly oozed out from between the slices of pressed bread. A towering bonfire of crispy fries was stacked beside the sandwich.

"God, that looks good. If I keep letting Nick cook for me, I'm going to gain a hundred pounds," Vivian said. "Nick is an incredible chef."

"You said that already." Della grinned, then took a bite of her sandwich, chewed and swallowed. "He's also a pretty incredible man. Any woman would be lucky to have him, if you ask me. Mavis and I have gotten to know him pretty well since he started working here."

Vivian avoided the obvious sell of Nick as a romantic prospect. This whole thing was a bump in the road, a short detour. As soon as possible, Vivian had to go back to the real world and that meant leaving that "incredible man" here in Stone Gap. The renovations on her apartment would be done soon, and then she could go back there. Get Ellie set up in the day care program at work, maybe hire a nanny for when she had to work late, and essentially go back to her normal life. Even if the idea of that sounded awfully stale right now. "Mavis knew his grandmother, she said."

Della nodded again. "Pretty much everyone in town knew Ida Mae. She was a big part of the Stone Gap community. Always organizing one thing or another, or helping out at things like the town picnic and the garden club. She's going to be sorely missed."

Despite Vivian's vow a second earlier to forget about Nick, curiosity nudged at her. "Did you know Nick when he was growing up?"

"No, not really. The Jackson boys lived in Raleigh, so they weren't in school with my three." Della grabbed a fry, dipped it in the cinnamon sauce, then popped it in her mouth. "I saw the boys with Ida Mae a few times when they visited her, and she'd take them down to the lake or over to the ice cream shop, but from what I gather, they liked to stay close to home during their visits. And with three of them, they could play together, so they didn't worry about making friends in the neighborhood. I did, however, get to know Nick's father. Regrettably."

"Why do you say that?"

"I know you're a lawyer, dear, and I'm sure you're a wonderful one. But Nick's father is…well, a bull-dog. If he was fighting for the underdog then I'd be fine with it, but he doesn't care who he's fighting for or against—he just wants to fight. He sued my husband's auto repair business for something that didn't need to go to court. Nearly bankrupted us, until Bobby went to the guy who filed the suit and worked it out in person. Those lawyers who go after businesses without knowing the whole story…" Della shook her head. "Well, I don't have anything nice to say about them."

Vivian nudged her trial paperwork to the side of the desk. She liked to think that she *did* fight for the underdog—Jerry certainly fit that description—but she knew she could be as ruthless as anyone in the courtroom, although Vivian's job was to make cold monolithic corporations pay for their mistakes and shortcuts. She wasn't trying to wipe out the neighbor's business. "I worked in an auto repair shop for a few months when I was young, doing little jobs mostly. One of my foster fathers owned a business like your husband's." Vivian had seen the sign for Gator's Garage on her way into town last week. She'd heard that Bobby Barlow was partially retired, and one of his sons was running the business now.

A business passed down from one generation to the next. If she'd had a child, would her son or daughter follow in her footsteps and go into law? Maybe come to work at the firm with Vivian some day? Or would her child be a rebel chef like Nick, carving out his or her own path?

"Well, should you ever need a job, Luke's always looking for extra hands at the garage." Della grinned.

"I'll keep that in mind." Vivian took a bite of her sandwich and swallowed. The flavors melted against her tongue, sweet and savory, all in one. "This is really good."

"Nick's amazing. We've had so many recent Yelp reviews raving about the cooking at the inn that we can hardly keep up with bookings. December's going to be crazy busy. Mavis and I never expected this little inn to take off so fast."

"I'm happy for both of you. It's a lovely place to stay."

"That's because Stone Gap is a lovely town to live in." Della dipped another fry in the cinnamon sauce. "Nick says you lived here briefly?"

Vivian had already finished off most of the sandwich and made a serious dent in the fries. No wonder people raved in reviews about the meals here. "I was only here for a couple months one summer, with my sister Sammie, Ellie's mother. We lived with a foster family. The Langstons."

"Oh, Ruth and John," Della said. "Lovely people. They must have fostered a hundred kids over the years. Opened their hearts and home to so many youngsters. They retired and moved to Arizona a couple years ago."

A regrettable fact that Vivian had learned after she booked the stay here, and looked up her former foster family. They'd had a pleasant phone conversation and made vague plans to meet up another time.

"It was the best foster home I ever stayed in." The only home where Vivian had imagined a real future, with family dinners around the dining room table and sleepovers with friends from school. From the day the girls stepped across the threshold of that blue-and-white ranch house, the Langstons had been warm and loving and had treated both girls like family. "I only wished I could have stayed longer."

"What happened that made you leave the Langstons? If you don't mind my asking." Della's eyes softened with true caring, and her hand covered Vivian's for a moment.

"The same story that happened over and over again in our lives." Vivian sighed. "Us girls were like a boomerang that pinged between my mother's house and wherever the state could find space for us. That summer, my mother got her act together enough to get custody of us again. We went back, but all her promises not to drink and to hold on to a job lasted about two weeks, and then we were taken away from her again and sent to the next home, and the one after that. Rinse and repeat. We bounced all over North Carolina. Sometimes Sammie and I were separated—not all homes want two teenage girls at the same time—but I managed to keep in touch with her, and sometimes got to go to the same school."

Sympathy shimmered in Della's eyes. "You poor things. All kids should have a proper home to grow up in. I just don't understand parents who can't put their children first."

Parents like Sammie, who had abandoned her daughter. Or like Vivian, who kept abdicating all the responsibilities to Nick, when Sammie had left her to be Ellie's parent. Did Della put them in that same category?

"So you and your sister are close?" Della asked. "She looked like a lovely girl when the two of you checked in. I'm sure being a single mom has been tough on her. I remember how overwhelming it was when I had my first son."

Vivian picked at the fries, her appetite gone. "Sammie and I grew apart after I turned eighteen and started living on my own. I booked the weekend here because I hoped it would be a chance for us to reconnect, in the one place where we both were happy for a short while. I didn't even know she'd had a baby until she showed up. And within twenty-four hours, she was gone again."

"And left her baby with you."

Vivian nodded.

"Poor girl must have been so desperate to do something like that," Della said. "Being a new mother is not an easy job. When my boys were little, there were many days when I thought about running away and joining the circus. Kids are a lot of work, and when you're a brand-new momma, you're always sure you are doing it wrong."

Or a brand-new aunt who had a thimbleful of parenting skills. "Maybe. But Sammie has never been super responsible anyway."

"Well, maybe she got scared when she realized little Ellie was counting on her to be responsible, and Sammie didn't quite know how to do that. Did I ever tell you about my early days with Jack?" Della shook her head and let out a little laugh. "Of course I haven't. We've only just met. But pretty much everyone around here knows what happened."

Vivian took a sip of her lemonade. "I can't imagine you ever being overwhelmed, Mrs. Barlow. You just seem so…capable of anything."

"Smoke and mirrors, sweetie, smoke and mirrors." Della pushed her plate to the side. "Jack was a fussy baby from the start, and I was a terribly nervous momma. My own mother was a good mother, but a little…distant. Not cold, just not warm, you know?"

Vivian nodded. She thought of Nick's parents. If Della had become a person who embraced everyone and made mothering look easy, then maybe Vivian would be able to do the same. Someday. Someday she would be somewhere else. And someday Nick would, too. Maybe he'd be with his own family with another woman. The thought made a sharp pain sear her chest.

"Anyway, there was one day when Jack just wouldn't stop crying. I'd gone maybe three, four days without sleep. That little booger was up all night, and both Bobby and I were exhausted. Jack was probably colicky, but I was so headstrong, I was sure I could handle this on my own, and that I didn't need to go to the doctor. Anyway, Bobby went to work, and I was home alone with little Jack. I tried everything. Blankets, bottles, binkies, walks, singing, rocking, offering him bribes—"

Vivian laughed. "I take it those didn't work?"

"Nothing worked. I felt like such a failure. So I decided I was going to just find someone else who could take care of Jack. I wasn't thinking of giving him away exactly…honestly, I'm not sure what I was thinking in my sleep-deprived mind. I was so convinced I was a terrible mother. I bundled Jack up and put him in the stroller and headed downtown. I was either going to find Mary Poppins or go see Bobby and have him help me somehow. I didn't even make it to the garage before Jack started crying so hard, I was worried he might choke. I stopped, sat down on a bench and just broke down."

"What happened?"

"Ida Mae, of all people, happened by. She sat down beside me and told me that her Richard had been the same way. A real pain in the butt, she said. That made me laugh, but I still couldn't stop crying." Della smiled at the memory. "I'm sitting there, holding my crying baby, and crying just as hard as he is. Sweet Ida Mae said, *here, let me*, in that soft, sweet way she had. She took that screaming little boy and rewrapped his blankets around him like a burrito."

"Swaddling." Nick had mentioned something about that the other day when he was holding Ellie. He had clearly inherited that soft, sweet way from his grandmother. "It calms the baby, right?"

"Yep. Makes them think they're all snug and happy in the womb again. Wouldn't you know, my little Jack stopped crying quick as a minute, and took his bottle like nothing had ever happened." Della pressed a hand to her heart. "Made me so happy. But then one second later, I felt like a failure all over again. I was his mom. I was supposed to know what he needed."

"I've felt the same way." The admission took a weight off Vivian's shoulders. If this capable, kind, smart woman had felt the same way with a new baby in her life, maybe it was more common than Vivian thought? "I'm a woman—aren't I supposed to be a natural mother?"

"I don't know if anyone is a natural mother. It's natural to love our kids the second they're born, of course, but we're also all scared to death we're going to screw them up. Most moms get past that, and realize that all they can do is their best and pray the good Lord directs their hand and watches over their kids."

"And some moms just keep on screwing up." Like her own mother.

Della gave a sad, slow nod. "They do, and they sometimes hurt their kids in the process. Not by intention, I don't believe, but like a car accident on the highway. A chain reaction. If you ask me, those moms are the ones who need the most love and understanding. They're struggling so very hard, and they still keep falling down."

"Like my sister. And my mother."

"Exactly. Just before she went on her way, Ida Mae said something to me that day that I've never forgotten. Something that got me through mothering three very active, very boisterous boys." Della leaned across the desk. "You can either choose to believe in yourself the way your baby does, or choose to believe the doubts that are whispering in your ear. From the day they were born, all my boys looked up at me and Bobby with love and trust. They believed we could take care of them and love them the way they deserved. It was up to us to rise to that challenge."

Undoubtedly, Vivian had looked at her own mother that way. There were days when her mother had been good—Vivian had spotty memories of doing puzzles and making sandwiches together—but then her mother would sink back into depression and self-medicating, and those days would end. Could it be that her mother had felt the same as Vivian and Della? Like a failure?

And every day she let her girls down again, she just proved her worst fears about herself?

"All your sister is hearing in her head are all those doubts," Della went on, "all those whispers that say she's not a good enough momma for Ellie. She's got to choose to believe differently." Della's concern and soft voice made it all sound so simple and clear. "Maybe Sammie truly isn't ready to be a parent right now and that's why Ellie is with you. Because it wouldn't be good for her to be a...what did you call it? Boomerang baby."

Vivian shook her head, and tried to ignore the flicker of guilt that she'd come very close to finding another home for Ellie. *Boomerang baby.* Just like she'd been and Sammie, too. "I'm no good at being a mother. I don't have the instincts for it."

"Oh, sweetie, you do too. We all do, if we choose to open our hearts." Della rose and picked up both plates. "Being a good mother starts with love. I've seen how you look at that baby. You have love in abundance. Start there. The rest will come. And give that little girl the kind of home and childhood you dreamed of having."

Then she left the office, leaving Vivian alone with Ellie, who had started to stir. No matter what Della Barlow said—or how cleverly she tried to convince Vivian to stay by mentioning jobs and what a wonderful place Stone Gap was to live in—Vivian knew the best option, for herself and for Ellie, was to stick with what she did best.

Being an island unto themselves.

* * *

The afternoon passed in a blur of emails, files, phone calls, diaper changes, bottles and visitors. The inn was a busy place during the day, guests in and out, meals served, housework done. The dining room was transformed for the impromptu birthday party for one of the guests, and the scent of cake fresh from the oven kept tempting Vivian out of the office. She tried to avoid Nick, but she found at least a half a dozen excuses to go into the kitchen. A glass of water. A paper towel to wipe up a spill. A new bottle for Ellie.

Every time, he greeted her with a smile that made her heart flip. As if he was genuinely glad for the interruption. They chatted a little, mostly small talk, then Vivian used the work excuse to duck back into the office.

She buried herself in the pages before her, the documents she was supposed to read. But it wasn't enough to forget Nick—

Or the big decisions that were waiting for her soon. Al had been the first to ask when she'd be back in the office full-time. "That court date is going to be here before you know it, Viv. We're going to need all hands on deck if any of this goes south before then."

She'd mumbled something vague, then hung up. Ellie, on her back in the playpen, was watching her hands wave back and forth. Happy, content, warm, fed. Looking up at her aunt with trust and belief. *You can either choose to believe in yourself the way your baby does, or choose to believe the doubts that are whispering in your ear.*

How could Vivian leave her? With the state, with a nanny, with anyone?

But how could she keep her? And do it all herself? Or manage to juggle motherhood and a busy career?

Vivian was just about to call the client with a status update when her phone rang. Sammie's number lit up the screen. Vivian nearly dropped the phone, fumbling to answer it. "Sammie. Where are you? Are you okay?"

"I'm fine." There was the sound of passing traffic behind Sammie's voice. "How's Ellie?"

Was her sister on a freeway? Hitchhiking? Frustration and anger trumped Vivian's concern in that moment, though. "She's fine. We've been watching her. What were you thinking, leaving her here?"

"Who's we?"

"Me and Nick, the chef at the inn. He's the one who found her in the kitchen. It's a long story. But she's fine." Then Vivian's anger ebbed, and her worry for her little sister returned. For so many years, it had been the two of them against a world that was always upside down. Outside, the air held a December chill, and Vivian wondered if her sister was cold, alone, hungry. "And you, you're okay?"

A horn blared. A beat passed. "Yes. I just…needed some time to clear my head."

Vivian bit off the first comment about being a responsible parent that came to mind. If she kept lashing out at her sister, it would only make Sammie more distant. "Where are you? Tell me, and I'll come get you."

"I'm okay," Sammie said. "I'm glad Ellie is with you. I…" Her voice caught. "I miss her so much, Viv."

"I know you do. I know you love her." Vivian pressed the phone tighter to her ear, as if she could transport through it to Sammie's side. "When are you coming back?"

"Soon. I promise." The traffic whipped by with a steady *vroom-vroom* sound. It had to be a highway. Vivian prayed Sammie wouldn't be stupid enough to hitchhike.

"I'll send you some money. Give me the address of where you're staying." Vivian readied a pen and dug through the pile on the desk for a blank sheet of paper.

But Sammie was already refusing. "I can't. Not yet. I… I wasn't ready to be a mom, and that's why I left. I've been going to counseling and working, and just trying to get my act together so I can be there for Ellie. I don't want to fail her like Mom did, you know? But I still don't know if I'm ready."

"You don't get a choice in that, Sammie. You have to grow up sometime. Ellie is here and she needs a mother."

"Who can be you until I'm ready."

"Sammie, I have a demanding job and a life in Durham. I can't be a mom, too." Vivian softened her tone. She thought of Nick's notes, of his soft, calm words that guided her through the simplest tasks with Ellie. "You can do this, I know you can."

"I'm not like you, Viv. I work as a waitress, and I barely pay my rent. I can't afford Ellie. And I sure can't afford day care while I work. You…you have money and a nice apartment and I'm sure you're so much better than I am with her. You were so good with me, Viv. A better mom than ours."

"Sammie, Ellie loves you. I've seen the two of you together. You're her mother, through and through. I'll help you with the money. Just come back. Please?"

"Take care of her for me, will you?" Sammie's voice broke. "I hate not being with her. But…I didn't know what else to do."

Damn it. Why wasn't Sammie listening? "Come back to Stone Gap. Ellie misses you."

Sammie's words caught on a sob. "I swore I'd never do this to my kids. Not after Mom did it to us."

In the space between them, a dozen memories flowed. The two girls, huddled together, sobbing, while strangers invaded their house yet again, piling their belongings into garbage bags while their mother ranted about the government. Being hungry, dirty, scared, but not wanting to leave. Not again. And then their mother, packing the rest of their things in the bags and shoving them out the door and turning her back on her daughters, a drink in her hand. Always a drink in her hand. "Then don't, Sammie. Please don't."

"You make it sound so easy. It's not, Viv. Babies need food and diapers and cribs and car seats, and all these things I can't afford."

"I'll buy all that. Call it early Christmas presents. I already shipped a bunch of things to your apartment a couple days ago." Vivian could hear the desperation in her voice, the hope that some money could smooth all these bumps for Sammie. She knew that was impractical, and a panacea for an unwieldly problem. But it was the best Vivian could offer.

There was a long moment of silence. "Do you really think I can be a good mom?"

"Yes, Sammie, I do."

"Maybe if I can get a better job, and find a better place to live—"

"Let me help you with that. I can pay—"

"I need to do those things on my own, Viv. I appreciate it, but like you said, I have to grow up sometime. And now is the time." Sammie sighed. "Just a few more days, okay?"

Vivian thought of the work week ahead of her. Nick was back at the inn during the days, which meant he wasn't going to be babysitting full-time anymore. He'd forced her to take a day off, which had been a nice break, she'd give him that, but it had put her even more behind. She needed to be in the office, not working from home. Otherwise, details got missed.

She was just going to have to contact her work's day care and find a nanny for after-hours. Go back to Durham this weekend, interview some caregivers and get a plan in place before Monday. Talk to her contractors and see if they could put a halt to the renovations and make the place livable by Monday. Staying here much longer only put her more behind at work. Maybe with the help of a nanny, she could at least leave the office at a reasonable time every day so she could spend time with her niece on a daily basis until Sammie returned.

"Yeah, sure. That'll be fine," Vivian said.

"Thanks, Viv. You're the best. I knew I could count on you."

As she hung up with her irresponsible little sister, Vivian realized she had just done the same thing she'd always done for Sammie—made escaping reality easier by taking away the pressures of real life.

Chapter Nine

Nick hadn't been this nervous in a long time. He finished the dinner shift at the inn, with Mavis and Della practically shoving him out the door so he could go home and get ready for his date that may or may not be a real date. He'd decided to treat it as a real date, regardless. Vivian might be all wrong for him, this always-working lawyer who had no interest in a family life, but the little glimpses he'd had of another side to her intrigued Nick. And as much as he tried to repress it, he couldn't deny that he was interested in her. Vivian had left a few minutes earlier, leaving Ellie with the two women. Della had Ellie in her arms, and was waiting for a bottle to warm.

"Don't you worry about a thing," Mavis said. "We are going to spoil this little girl rotten, and keep her up well past her bedtime."

Nick chuckled and gathered up his bag. "I have no doubt you will. All right. We'll be back by nine to pick her up."

When he pulled in the driveway of Ida Mae's, he did a double take. The lights were on, drenching the windows with a soft golden glow, and the soft strains of the radio could be heard when he stepped out of the pickup. Some Frank Sinatra song. Nick could see the Christmas decorations he'd put up in the days before, looking bright and festive and homey. Welcoming.

For a second, he was ten years old and running into his grandmother's house, rushing toward the sight of warm cookies and even warmer hugs. This house, with its lilac shutters and ring of rosebushes, was home, Nick realized, more than any home he'd ever known.

He pulled out his cell and called Grady. "Hey, big brother. When are you coming down here to see your inheritance?"

"Work is crazy," Grady said into the phone, then he gave directions to someone driving. "I'm heading into a meeting in a minute. I thought you said you were staying in the house. The electric and gas are all paid. And I'll send a maintenance guy by every month to check on any necessary repairs."

In other words, Grady was going to be as hands-off about his inheritance as Nick was about the box. He wondered what that said about the two of them. "I am staying here. But the house is technically yours. Which means I think I'll have to look for one of my own."

"What, down there? In Stone Gap?" Grady scoffed.

"I know you loved that place but the only good thing about it to me was Grandma."

"There's more good here than you know." Was Nick talking about the weather? The inn? Or maybe a certain woman he was seeing tonight?

"Well, feel free to stay there as long as you like," Grady said. "I miss you, brother."

"Miss you too. Come down and visit sometime."

Grady scoffed. "Chances of that are slim. Talk to you later."

Grady hung up and Nick realized that telling his brother to come and visit sometime implied he wasn't going anywhere. He'd thought his move to Stone Gap was temporary, but as he stood there in Ida Mae's driveway, he realized he didn't want to leave this place, a town that held all his best memories. The job at the inn might not be glamorous or even pay all that well, but it was a job where he felt content, where he created things that made people happy. And that was something he'd been seeking all his life. He was going to take Grady up on his offer, and stay in the house until he found one of his own.

Nick got out of the car, took the porch stairs two at a time, then walked inside. "Honey, I'm home!"

The joke echoed into an empty space. He checked the living room, then the kitchen. No Vivian. As he returned to the hallway, he heard the sound of her heels on the wooden staircase. He watched Vivian descend, giving him a slow reveal of long, long, amazing legs, a sleek black dress and sexy shoulders bared by her upswept hair.

"Holy cow. You look…" He turned to the small bookcase in the hall and feigned grabbing a book. "Wait, let me get the thesaurus, because amazing isn't a good enough word for how you look."

She laughed and stopped on the last step. A faint blush filled her cheeks. He liked that blush. And loved that he was the one who caused it.

"This is probably too much for dinner and tree shopping," she said, "but my wardrobe consists mainly of the things I've brought back from my apartment over the past few days, and the things I brought with me for the weekend with Sammie—so basically, court suits, jeans and this one dress in case Sammie and I went out."

"It's perfect." He leaned over and kissed her cheek, drawing in a whisper of her fragrance, a bit of her warmth. He wanted to draw her close, to touch all the enticing parts bared by the dress. Later, he hoped, there would be time for that. "Give me five minutes and let me see if I can find something that does that dress justice."

A tease quirked her lips. "Should I time you?"

He slipped off his watch and pressed it into her hands. "If I don't make it in time, then how about… I owe you another night on the town?"

She parked a fist on her hip. "And how is that a prize for me?"

"Hopefully, you'll see tonight." He gave her a quick kiss, then took the stairs two at a time, peeling off his shirt as he headed for the shower, and getting ready in record time. He opted for a pale blue button-down shirt and a dark patterned tie under the suit he'd worn for Ida Mae's funeral. Like Vivian, he hadn't packed much beyond the essentials. At the inn, he didn't have to get any fancier than jeans and a polo shirt. The few extra pieces he'd needed in the last month, he'd bought locally. At some point he had to go back to his apartment and clean it out, he supposed. The thought didn't depress him anymore and in fact, he was looking forward to finding a little house of his own here in town. Except to have the money to do that, he had to fulfill Ida Mae's request. That thought *did* depress him. Maybe he should just put the damned box in the mail and be done with it. Until then, there was tonight. And Vivian. And that sexy black dress.

He charged down the stairs and feigned panting, his hands on his knees. "Whew! That was tough. Did I make it?"

"Five minutes and twenty-seven seconds." She gave him back his watch. "I think you did that on purpose."

"I may have." He grinned, then put out his arm. "Your dinner awaits, milady." He took her out to the pickup, held the door and helped her up into the seat. She'd put a long coat over the dress, and the suede slid across his leather seat with a slight whoosh. "Sorry we aren't riding in something fancier, but the truck is the most practical for Christmas tree shopping."

"I'm not a fancy kind of girl, Nick," she said. "I like a simple life. I really do."

He was counting on that tonight, and had wagered his idea for a date would be perfect for the Vivian he knew. Not harsh, commanding courtroom Vivian, but the barefoot in the dark Vivian he liked very, very much. He put the truck in gear, swung out of the driveway, then took a left on Lakeshore Road.

"We aren't going into town?"

"Later, when we get the tree. But for now, I wanted to take you somewhere special." The road curved around the perimeter of the lake, winding down past the Sea Shanty, which was lit but sparsely populated on this early winter night, and then came to an end at a park that had seen better days. The town still decorated it for the holidays, though, and dozens of white lights greeted them as Nick pulled into the parking lot and shut the truck off. The engine ticked as it cooled, the only sound in the quiet night.

Vivian drew in a breath. "Wow. This looks so beautiful."

There were lights all over, but a particularly large concentration had been woven along the posts and between the rafters of a white-and-dark-green gazebo, as if God had dropped a constellation in the middle of the park. The reflection of the decorations twinkled on the dark lake, undisturbed save for the occasional splash of a rushing fish. Swags of evergreens looped around the railings, caught with giant red bows at each pillar.

Nick got out of the truck, came around, opened the passenger door, and extended a hand for Vivian. "You can leave your coat in the truck."

"It's cold out, though."

"Trust me, Vivian."

She shrugged out of the long garment and set it on the seat. "I rarely trust anyone."

"I know. Come see for yourself." As she stepped down, he grabbed the basket he'd packed earlier. She gave him an inquisitive glance, but didn't say anything as he led her up the crushed shell walkway, one arm around her, supposedly to block the faint breeze off the lake, but considering it was warm, he knew, as she probably did too, that he was using the kiss of wind as an excuse to touch her. Three steps up to the gazebo's entrance, and Vivian paused.

"Oh, Nick." She turned to him, a hand to her lips, her eyes shimmering. "That is the sweetest thing anyone has ever done."

His heart jumped and he had the craziest urge to cry. The joy and surprise in her face could have knocked him over. He cleared his throat. "Now don't go getting all emotional on me. It's just some blankets and a ceramic heater." He led her to the cushions he'd borrowed from the inn's outdoor furniture, then fished a lighter and a big candle out of the basket and lit it.

"How did you…where did you…?"

"I borrowed the heater from Jack Barlow when I got this crazy idea this afternoon. Ran up here and set all this up on my way home from the inn. It wasn't much. Really." Because the way she was looking at him made Nick feel like he could have done so much more to earn the tears brimming in her eyes.

Vivian shook her head. "No, it's perfect. It's truly perfect. And warm, like you said."

He uncorked a bottle of white wine he'd kept chilled in the basket, then poured them each a glass. "I'm glad you like it. We could have gone to a restaurant, but I thought we both could use a night…"

"Alone."

He shrugged, because that one word held connotations Nick wasn't sure either of them was ready to address. Instead, he sat down on the opposite cushion and began unloading the basket. "Chicken marsala, with whipped Parmesan potatoes and Italian peas with roasted pearl onions. And…homemade Parker House rolls."

"You know my weaknesses well, Mr. Jackson."

"I hope that one of them is me." He tucked a lock of hair behind her ear and allowed his hand to linger on her jaw. "And that is, without a doubt, the corniest thing I've ever said."

"I didn't think it was corny." Deep blue pools met his gaze, as dark and mysterious as the depths of Stone Gap Lake. "Not at all."

She leaned forward, and the shifting of her weight on the cushion made her slide into him. He didn't complain. Nick slipped an arm around Vivian and lifted her onto his lap. She laughed and wrapped her arms around his neck. "What are we doing?"

"Enjoying our appetizer." He nibbled at her neck, then down the curve of her dress to the swell of her breasts. She arched into him, her hands tangling in his hair. Their breath was short, their hearts racing, and everything within him wanted to lay her down on those cushions and make love to her until the sun came up. Instead, Nick drew back and pressed his forehead to hers. "If we keep that up, we'll never have dinner."

"Or dessert."

"So, do we eat first? Then make out?"

She laughed and slid off his lap, then settled on the cushion, in prim and proper form. "Yes. I do think that's wise."

He did, too, but not because he was hungry. Because he knew that he wasn't just falling for this town, and thinking about something more permanent here. He was falling for Vivian, too. The vulnerability she struggled so hard to contain, the strength and smarts that had gotten her from foster homes to multimillion-dollar lawsuits. The fierce love and loyalty she felt for her family, her sister.

And the way she kissed him. For the first time in a long time, Nick realized what it was like to be with someone who had no other someones in mind. Whose sole attention was on him, with a warmth and connection that he hadn't realized he'd been missing until he had it.

If he was going to make this work, then he had to do it right, and that meant not rushing headlong into a relationship. That was the kind of thing that would make Vivian bolt. And besides, there were questions he had to answer for himself, too. Like how much he was willing to compromise when it came to her work situation.

He put his phone on some soft jazz background music, dished up the food and for a while they exchanged small talk about Ellie, the inn, the town, the weather. The words flowed between them on a companionable river, light and easy as leaves skimming the surface.

"So, what's your plan for this Christmas tree we are buying later?" she asked.

"I don't have a plan. It can be whatever we want. I'm not one of those 'everything must match and look like it came out of *Architectural Digest*' kind of people. I'm pretty much a go-with-my-gut guy. Which works well in cooking, not so well in designing security code for computers."

She laughed. "I can see that. That's a job where everything has to follow precise directions, I'm sure. As for me, I've had everything mapped out for my life for so long, I'm not sure I have the ability to go with my gut."

He mixed some chicken with the potatoes and swallowed the morsel. "Isn't that exactly what you have to do when you're raising a kid who can't speak yet?"

"I'd say I'm just following your lead and hoping I don't screw up." She took a sip of wine, then set the glass on the wooden floor of the gazebo. The twinkling lights woven into the rafters bounced off the goblet. "Although today went much better than I expected. It helped that Mavis and Della were in the office every five minutes to hold Ellie."

"You're better with Ellie than you think," Nick said. "When you loosen up the bun and the rules, you're calm and that's contagious to everyone around you."

"Loosen up the bun?" She laughed a little, then sat back on her elbows. "What does that mean?"

"Well, there are two Vivians. Courtroom Vivian,

with the bun and the suits, and late at night home Vivian, when you quit working and take a breath. The Vivian with the bright red nail polish and the smile that lights up a room." He toyed with a lock of her hair. The easy updo she had tonight meant a few tendrils framed her face, dusted her neck. "That's the beautiful Vivian I can't resist."

"You can't?" she asked, the words breathless and hushed.

"Not from the minute you came storming into the inn."

"And you threatened to call the police on me."

"Well, I thought you were a babynapper."

"Do I look like a babynapper?"

He pretended to study her, tilting his head left, right, tapping a finger on his chin, until she laughed. "Nope. You look like a woman I would enjoy spending time with."

"Well, when you find that woman, you might want to spend some time with her."

That earned a laugh out of Nick. "Touché. I think I've met my match. You are pretty damned smart, Vivian." He shifted closer to her. The scent of her perfume warmed the space between them. "In case you're keeping track, that's two compliments in the space of five minutes."

That flush filled her cheeks again. "I noticed."

"I must say, I'm feeling quite unappreciated." He feigned outrage and put a hand on his chest. "Every night this week, you have come home to dinner made,

kid bathed and ready for bed, and a bevy of compliments—"

"I'd hardly call two a bevy."

"And what do I receive for my efforts? An 'I noticed.' Humph."

She laughed. "You do know that you sound like a
nagging wife, right now, don't you?"

"Considering I've never had a wife, I wouldn't
know."

"Why not?" She put a little distance between them
and took another bite of dinner. "Why haven't you
been married?"

"I could ask you the same thing. You're a beautiful
woman, and I can't imagine why you're still single."

"Will you quit calling me beautiful?" She ducked
her head, and he swore he saw another blush on her
face. "Besides, I asked you first."

He paused a moment, thinking about his answer.
He'd never really given the subject much thought.
Even the decision to propose to Ariel had been a more
of a this-is-the-logical-next-step thing "I avoided anything that had the potential to become a long-term relationship most of my life. My parents had such an
awful marriage, and I didn't want to end up like them.
From what I heard, my grandparents had a perfect
marriage, but after my grandpa died when my dad
was a teenager, people said Ida Mae was never quite
the same again." Grandma Ida Mae had kept her late
Henry's portrait on the mantel, and hanging in the
hallway. She'd stop and talk to it sometimes, her un-
dying love clear in her voice. Even as a kid, Nick had

understood that pain, that deep, abiding emotion, and the fragility of it all. "I guess I didn't want to take a chance on having something that good and losing it."

"I understand that." She sighed and took another sip of wine, then waved off his offer of a refill. "I've spent my entire life not counting on good things. Every time my life seemed to be on track, I'd end up yanked out of that house and sent to another, or I'd be moved to another school or Sammie would get in trouble and I'd have to go run and help her."

"And you learned not to rely on anyone but yourself?"

"Exactly."

"Sounds like we're two peas in a pod," he said. He set down his half-empty wineglass. "And maybe I should do the same, considering the first woman I thought about marrying ran off with my supposed best friend."

"But you seem to fit into the two-point-five kids, dog in the yard life and all of this—" she waved a hand around the gazebo, past the lake, toward the town and the life that existed just around that bend "—so easily. You created a home in a vacant house in a few days, Nick. I haven't been able to do that in thirty years."

"All I did was build on the home my grandmother had. She was the one who did all these things—set up the Christmas tree, baked the cookies, read us stories at bedtime. My parents hired nannies and chauffeurs and paid people to raise us, essentially." He had, indeed, re-created his memories in the way he'd decorated the house for Christmas. The stuffed Santa was in the same place on the sofa, the candles and evergreen bows displayed as they always had been. Grady, he knew, wouldn't have cared if Nick redecorated the whole house. Grady clearly had no intentions of living there, and no intentions of returning to Stone Gap. Grady would keep up the maintenance of Ida Mae's house, but otherwise ignore his inheritance. Nick wanted to have one last holiday there, even if the rooms echoed a little too much now.

"So you spent your childhood with strangers, too, in a way," Vivian said.

Strangers. That was a good word for the paid help who'd raised him, and for his parents, especially his father. They'd never seen eye to eye, never had a single thing in common. Why Ida Mae had tasked Nick with reconnecting with Richard, Nick had no idea. Of the three Jackson boys, he was the least likely candidate. Even though none of them had become lawyers, at least his older brothers were both successful, driven, hard-chargers like their father. Nick was far more content with his low-stress, low-ambition chef's life in Stone Gap. The direct opposite of his father. Maybe that was part of Ida Mae's thinking. "Guess that whole living with strangers thing might be another part of the reason neither one of us have settled down."

She scoffed. "Boy, we'd make some therapist rich if we ever decided to unpack our emotional baggage."

"That's very true. Here's to us." He raised his wineglass, and she did the same. A merry clink sounded in the quiet night. "Now all that aside, we have yet to settle our debate."

"What debate is that?" She took another bite, and he could tell by the smile on her face that the dinner was a hit. He'd made hundreds of dinners, but never had he been so committed to making a diner happy as he had with Vivian.

"Whether or not you appreciate me, especially after my bevy of compliments." Nick grinned.

She rolled her eyes and laughed. "Okay, you want a compliment?"

"Why yes, I do."

Vivian glanced around the space. Her gaze skipped over the thick blankets, the ceramic heater, the basket and the spread of food, now almost entirely gone. "You...cook very well."

"Well now there, Ms. Winthrop, be careful because you're getting awful personal."

She pursed her lips but her eyes danced with merriment, and Nick decided this was his favorite Vivian, the one who laughed and teased. "Okay, so you're also...pretty good-looking."

"Be still, my heart." He put a hand on his chest. "I may have to put that in my next online dating profile. Should bring the ladies running. Cooks well and is pretty good-looking."

"And you know it. So there, that's the end of my compliments." She raised her chin and met his gaze.

"Too bad. Because now I'll never know..." He raised up on his knees and leaned toward her.

She watched him, her eyes wide. A breath passed between them. The lights sparkled on her face, danced golden dust on her eyelashes. "Never know what?"

"If you want me to kiss you again."

A loon called across the lake in the distance. A soft splash spoke of a fish being chased. Clouds drifted past the moon, casting a hazy veil over the world.

"Well, I...well..." She swallowed, then let out a breath, and one whispered word. "Yes."

Instead of kissing her right away, Nick got to his feet, put out his hands, then drew Vivian up and into his arms. The radio shifted to a slow song, as if the DJ was in on some kind of a conspiracy to bring them together. Nick put one hand on Vivian's waist, took her opposite hand with his, then began to waltz her away from the blankets and the heater and into the center of the gazebo. She kicked off her heels, and danced barefoot on the painted wood.

With her shoes off, she was a few inches shorter than him, but she fit against him as if she had been made for the space between his arms. A couple of missteps, and then their rhythms synced. He leaned closer, inhaling the dark scent of her perfume. Like Vivian herself, even her perfume had layers and surprises.

A few more renegade tendrils had escaped the updo and skated along the edge of her neck. He whispered a kiss just below them, as light as a breeze. Then another and another, dancing down her neck with his lips. She let out a soft gasp, and her hand tightened in his. Her eyes widened in the low interior light. "What are we doing?"

"Dancing. Kissing. Mostly dancing."

"It feels a lot like something more."

"Yes, it does." What more, he didn't want to voice,

afraid the moment was as fragile as a soap bubble. Instead, he stopped moving, cupped her face in his hands, and kissed Vivian good and proper. The way he'd wanted to since the day he met her.

She leaned into him, her hold tightening. The music shifted to something else, but neither of them noticed. They had this moment, and neither wanted to let it go.

Chapter Ten

Dozens of Christmas trees lined the tarred parking lot of the white Presbyterian church in downtown Stone Gap. One wizened old man in a Charlotte Hornets ball cap and a flannel shirt manned the lot. A bright orange pair of work gloves waved from the back pocket of his worn jeans. "Merry Christmas! Can I help you two lovebirds find a tree?"

Lovebirds?

Then Vivian realized she'd been holding hands with Nick ever since she'd gotten out of the truck. Actually she hadn't stopped touching him ever since they left the gazebo. They'd danced and kissed until the air got too cold, and they had to pack up the food and leave. She could blame it all on the wine, but she'd only had one glass, and Nick hadn't even finished his. The dancing, the kissing, the hand-holding, had all been...

Wonderful.

If she was honest with herself, that's what she'd say. Wonderful and sweet and temporary. She'd expected Nick to be like every other man she'd dated—men who took her to nice restaurants and said nice things, but left as much of an impression as a drop of water on a sponge. The romantic gazebo setting, the thoughtfulness of the heater, the amazing meal and ambiance had all been the kind of moments she would hold on to long after she left Stone Gap.

And that's what she needed to remember. No matter how wonderful their date had been, no matter how much she wished they'd done more than kiss and dance tonight, this was a single date that was coming to its inevitable end. She had yet to tell Nick she planned to go back to Durham this weekend because she kept getting distracted from her job and her situation with Ellie by this man. She had maybe twenty-four hours left in this fantasy bubble of Stone Gap and Nick Jackson before her real life returned. Selfishly, she didn't want their time together to end yet, but she also knew the sooner she stopped being so attached, the easier leaving would be.

She released his hand and stepped away, drawing her coat tighter as an excuse to let go of Nick. A chill chased along her empty palm. "Just a simple tree," she said to the man. "Nothing fancy."

The older man thrust out his hand. "Name's Cutler Shay. Welcome to Stone Gap."

"How do you know I'm from out of town?" Vivian asked.

"I've been around Stone Gap long enough to know pretty much every man, woman, child and grandchild in these parts. You don't look one bit familiar, so I'm guessing you're an out-of-towner. But you…" He stepped toward Nick and studied his face for a moment. "You're… one of Ida Mae's grandsons, aren't you? You've got her nose and her eyes, my boy."

"I am. I'm Nick. The youngest of the three." Nick shook his head. "Wow. I'm surprised you'd recognize me."

"Oh, I'm not that good." Cutler waved off the words. "Just joshing with you. I saw you moving into your grandmother's house. I live across the street. And scuttlebutt around town is that you've been settling in here, working at the Stone Gap Inn."

Nick grinned. "Of course. The Stone Gap gossip chain. Nice to see you again, Mr. Shay."

"Cutler will do just fine. Any relative of Ida Mae's is a friend of mine." He gave each of them a grin, then made a sweeping gesture of the lot. Trees lined either side of a pathway that extended from the front of the church to the back, all along the side driveway. Three-inch white Christmas bulbs strung between the trees to separate them somewhat into aisles provided decent enough lighting to see the trees, and hand-lettered bright red and white tags showed the pricing up front. "You might want to look at one of the Douglas firs. Ida Mae was always partial to them, and they look mighty nice in that corner of her living room. How long are you living there? Might want to get a watering system if you're staying past the holidays."

Vivian glanced at Nick, then back at Cutler. "It's just a temporary thing."

"Uh-huh. I've heard that before." Cutler started walking through the tree lot, passing the squat blue spruces, the plump Norway spruces and the skinny traditional pines as he spoke. "You know, your grandmother and grandfather, God rest their souls, said the same thing when they first bought that house."

"I thought my grandmother always lived here in town."

"She did. Like me, she grew up in Stone Gap, and like most of us when we hit eighteen, she said she was going to move to somewhere bigger and fancier after we graduated. Living in Stone Gap was only a 'temporary thing.'" Cutler's wrinkled hands fashioned air quotes around his words. He paused by a selection of Douglas firs and raised a caterpillar brow in Vivian's direction. "But this town has a way of growing on you when you're not looking."

Why was everyone trying to sell her on Stone Gap as a home? She had a life elsewhere, a job, an apartment. Her time here was all going to be done and over in a day or two. "Yeah, like moss on a tree."

Cutler laughed. "Yeah, like moss. But you know, moss serves a purpose. It helps the tree retain water, save it up for those days that are dry and hot as Hades. At first, the tree might be annoyed by the moss, but after a while, it realizes the moss gives the tree a better life."

Vivian didn't quite see how that equated to moving to a tiny town in North Carolina, but she wasn't about to argue. Cutler seemed to be full of homilies, and right now, she just wanted to get the tree and go. This night with Nick was making her want things she couldn't have. Best to end it quick, with this one last memory. "All these trees look great. Can you just wrap one up for us?"

"Now, now, you can't just pick a tree like that. A Christmas tree is special. It needs to be chosen by the people who are putting it up. It's going to be a part of your home—" Cutler put up a hand "—temporary or not, doesn't matter a whit. You should always make sure the tree feels like part of your family."

A part of their family? It was just a tree. And they were not a family. Not even close. Even if Nick saw it that way. The words panicked her because a part of her had long ago stopped believing she could have the very thing that she'd lacked all her life.

Vivian looked at Nick. He shrugged and gave her a grin, unfazed.

"Now, the Douglas fir isn't exactly a fir. You see these cones here?" Cutler reached in between the branches to point out one of the long brown cones. "They're distinctive just to the Douglas firs. This French botanist some years back—and his name is all Frenchie, so I can't pronounce it—named the Douglas fir a 'false hemlock,' because it looks like one of those trees. But don't worry, it's not the kind of hemlock that Socrates used to poison himself. Or was it Plato?"

Cutler shook his head. "That's neither here nor there. What's important is which of these trees feels right?"

To Vivian, every one of the bright green trees with their dark brown cones looked exactly the same. Okay, yes, she could tell that a few sat wide and short, others were taller and leaner. But tree for tree, they were nearly indistinguishable. Cutler was staring at her, though, with a grin on his face that was half-knowing and half-expectant, so she pointed to the tree on her right. "That one." She turned to Nick. "Does that work for you?"

"Yep. Seems like the perfect tree for us. A little lopsided and in need of a good home."

Lopsided? She hadn't noticed that. But as Cutler pulled the tree out from among the others, she saw that the one she'd chosen did, indeed, lean a bit to the left. "Are you sure you want a tree that's not perfect?" she asked Nick.

"None of us are perfect, Vivian," he said. "You can look at that tree, or that one, and you'll find a flaw. The flaws are what make the trees interesting, though. And people, for that matter."

Good Lord. Cutler was rubbing off on Nick. But why was it that when Nick talked, all Vivian could do was stare into his dark brown eyes and listen to the cadence of his words? The wine. It had to be the wine.

A single glass of a fruity chardonnay affecting her that deeply? Unlikely. More that she'd grown to like Nick. Very much. That was all. He was a good friend. An interesting man.

An interesting man who could kiss her and make her forget everything and everyone else. An interesting man who touched her and made her melt. An interesting man who wasn't going to be so easy to leave behind.

Cutler cleared his throat. "All right, kids, let me wrap her up and get her ready for you. Then you can go home, put on the Christmas carols and get decorating." Cutler took the tree with him as Nick and Vivian followed, then he laid it on a wrapping machine and pushed a button. Orange netting slipped around the tree, pressing it into a more easily transportable shape. "After we finished decorating the tree, my wife and I, God rest her soul, would sit on the couch and watch the lights twinkle. I used to think she was a sentimental fool, but now that she's gone, I realized I was the fool for not paying more attention."

A brisk breeze whistled through the lot, as if in answer to his words. Love and devotion weighted the ends of Cutler's words, and shimmered in his eyes. He raised his gaze to the sky for a moment, then gave a little cough and bent to tie some twine around the base of the tree. "Damn, I miss her. Should have appreciated her more when she was by my side."

"I'm so sorry about your wife," Vivian said. What would it be like to be loved that much? Or to give that kind of love to another? The kind of love that transcended life and death, and lingered in your veins?

"Aw, thank you, miss. My Sarah was a saint for putting up with me. And when you find a keeper like that, you don't let go." Cutler straightened and took the cash from Nick. "Doesn't matter where you live or what you live in. The right woman is the one who makes it a home. Remember that, son."

"I will," Nick said. "You have a good Christmas, Cutler." He hoisted the tree onto one shoulder and headed back to the pickup truck, sliding the tree into the bed in one smooth move. He opened the door for Vivian and helped her up.

Their touch extended a few seconds longer than necessary. His hand warmed hers, and his gaze filled her with a comfortable joy she had never known. If only a bottle existed that could hold this moment, so that when she returned to Durham she could revisit Nick's touch from time to time. "We, uh, should pick up Ellie and get that tree set up before it gets too late."

Nick dropped her hand and stepped back. "You're right. We should." Then he closed the door and walked around to the driver's side. The drive to the Stone Gap Inn only took a few minutes, but the bubble that had wrapped around them from the minute she'd come down the stairs in her dress had popped, and they were back to being simply strangers who'd formed a temporary alliance to help one little baby feel safe and protected.

Mavis and Della almost didn't want to give Ellie back. "She is just the cutest thing," Mavis said, with Ellie in her arms, swaddled in a pink blanket and already dressed in her pajamas. "Such a good baby."

Della ran her finger over Ellie's tiny hand and gave the baby a smile. "My boys were never that sweet.

They cried so much, I've always told them I would have given them back if they weren't so darn cute."

Nick laughed. "If I promise to bring her back, will you let us take her home and put her to bed?"

Mavis made a face of discontent, but handed Ellie over. "You make sure to tell her that her aunties Mavis and Della can't wait to spoil her again."

"And that we'll bake her cookies soon as she starts getting a couple teeth." Della tapped Ellie's chin. "Isn't that right? Any kind of cookies you want, sugar pie."

"We better get out of here before they build her a swing set in the yard," Nick muttered to Vivian. She'd said maybe three words to him on the short ride from the church to the inn, and had found ways to avoid his touch. After the wonderful time they'd had in the gazebo—most of all, the way she had responded when he kissed her—Nick wondered where things had gone left instead of right. Had he said something that made her mad? Things had changed after the Christmas tree purchase, and he was damned if he knew why.

"Thank you so much for watching her." Vivian gathered up the diaper bag while Nick put Ellie in the baby carrier. Vivian headed out the door first, but Della pulled Nick aside just before he left.

"How did it go tonight?" she whispered.

Della had helped him coordinate the heater with Jack, and had lent him the insulated basket for the food and wine. Probably out of some misguided plan to make Nick and Vivian fall in love and settle down in Stone Gap with Ellie, the newly adopted granddaughter of the Stone Gap Inn. He couldn't bear to tell Della that the evening was ending on a flat note. "Pretty good."

Della smiled. "She seems like a very sweet woman when you get her away from working. I had a lovely conversation with her this afternoon, you know. About babies, motherhood, and you."

About him? Nick wanted to ask what Vivian had said, but that would have been obvious and needy, and he was neither.

"I agree," Mavis said. "I've seen how that girl looks at you, Nick. She's more smitten than she realizes."

The two women couldn't have been more blatant matchmakers if they'd been holding up signs. Nick bit back a groan. "I'll see you tomorrow morning, ladies. Thanks again."

"No worries. It was our pleasure." Della gave Ellie a quick kiss on the forehead. "See you tomorrow."

Nick started out the door again, but Mavis stopped him with a touch on his shoulder. "One more thing." Cold air was coming through the open door, and he could see Vivian sitting in the truck, but Mavis paid neither any attention. "I heard your father will be in town tomorrow."

"Why? And how did you hear that?"

"I have a little birdie down at the town hall. He said your dad is coming into town to meet with a client about a new building project that's getting some pushback from the commissioners."

"That's a lot of words for a little birdie." There had been talk about a small outdoor mall going up in Stone Gap, something many people in the town opposed because they believed it would ruin the character and charm of the area. Some corporation had apparently looked at Stone Gap's location off of Route 95 and decided it was perfect for more tourism. Nick wasn't surprised his bulldog father was involved in the legal battle over that.

"Just call him. Meet him for lunch. Like Ida Mae asked you to." Mavis's features softened. "Your grandmother wouldn't have asked if she didn't think it was important. For you *and* her only son."

Ida Mae's only son had barely stayed to the end of his own mother's funeral. He'd let her grandsons handle the arrangements, contributing only by handing Grady a check. *Just tell me the time and date*, their father had said. Ida Mae leaving the house to Grady rather than Richard wasn't a big surprise—over the years the Jacksons had made millions from their law firm. They hardly needed more property when they already owned the Mausoleum and multiple vacation homes all over the world. Instead, she'd left her son and daughter-in-law some stocks, her other grandsons money equal to the house she'd left Grady, and then that damnable box that Nick had yet to deal with. And a not-so-simple request for Nick.

"I'll…think about it." Then he said goodbye for the hundredth time and stepped out into the chilly air.

Ellie was completely worn out by her adventurous day at the inn, and fell asleep as soon as the truck started. Vivian had hoped for some baby distraction tonight, but Ellie went straight to bed, barely stirring when they got home and Nick carried her upstairs.

Vivian followed him up to the nursery. Ellie's tiny head was nestled into Nick's shoulder, and soft baby snores escaped with her breaths. Nick paused by the crib, cupping Ellie's head as he lowered her onto the mattress. Every move he made with the baby held tenderness.

It almost made Vivian jealous. What would it be like for Nick to touch her that way?

He stood beside the crib and smiled down at Ellie. "She really is a beautiful baby," he said quietly. "And so well behaved. Not that I have any other babies to compare her to."

Vivian shifted to stand by Nick. She held the railing, her hands close enough to touch his. Ellie's eyelashes fluttered, and every once in a while one of her hands would clench and unclench, as if she was holding something in her dreams.

A beam of moonlight speared into the carpet, reflecting off Ellie's delicate features and then the dancing horses mobile above her head. On the scarred maple dresser, the short night-light matched the moon with a silvery pool of light. The carpet beneath their feet was soft and thick.

All across America, new parents were doing this same thing. Standing in a dim nursery, watching their sleeping baby, a little universe of just the three of them. If she and Nick were married, she could, for a split second, imagine that this was their life. Their family.

Her heart filled, a rush of emotion so strong, tears

threatened her eyes and her throat thickened. Vivian Winthrop had gone most of her life trying not to make connections, because she'd learned early on that the love of others could disappear as quickly as a storm cloud. She didn't get attached, didn't start to care, didn't let her heart open. Until this week with Nick and Ellie.

He'd made her believe in things she'd convinced herself were fictional. And worse, he'd made her want those very things for herself.

"She really is beautiful," Vivian whispered. "And impossible not to love."

"If she were ours…" Nick began, then shook his head, as if speaking the words aloud would create something he didn't want to breathe to life.

"Yeah," Vivian said. "But she isn't."

His hand slid over to cover hers. His fingers were warm, strong. "I never realized how much I was missing out on until you and Ellie came into my life."

"I was thinking the same thing just now." She turned to face him. Maybe it was the dim light, or the moment, or the dinner date, but for just tonight, Vivian didn't want to be her usual cautious, closed-off self. *If you stay with me, it gives me an excuse to hang some lights and make some eggnog and cookies and have the kind of holiday normal people have*, Nick had said a week ago. She had gone along with the plan then, mostly out of desperation. Now, they had a tree in the back of the truck and a box of decorations to hang, and the rest of the wine to drink while Christmas carols played in the background. "Tonight, Nick, let's just pretend."

"Pretend what?"

"That…this is our baby, and our first Christmas and…that there's an us." That he wasn't with her out of an agreement or because of Ellie, but because he wanted her and wanted to be with her forever.

"I think that's a great idea because I really want there to be an us right now," he said. Nick leaned over and kissed her, then took her hand, and the two of them headed downstairs. While she put on the radio and poured the wine, Nick brought in the tree.

She held the door for him, ushering in a chilly breeze. Vivian had yet to change out of her dress, and she stood in the doorway, shivering. "Hurry up. It's cold out here."

"I can't believe that because you're looking mighty hot."

She rolled her eyes. "Okay, now *that's* the corniest thing you've ever said." But she laughed anyway, as the tree spearheaded the way down the hall, and Nick pressed another quick kiss to her lips as he passed by.

Bing Crosby was singing "White Christmas" on the radio as Nick set the tree into the stand in the living room, then pulled out a pocketknife and cut off the netting. The branches sprung out, casting a spray of needles on the floor. Nick adjusted the stand, pulling it away from the wall to give the tree more room. "Do you want me to straighten it so it doesn't look so lopsided?"

Vivian shook her head. "You're right. It's better because it's not perfect." This entire week with Ellie had been imperfect, filled with a couple bumps and detours, and yet, right now, Vivian wouldn't change a thing. The forced day off and the time with the baby had begun to loosen the bonds and expectations that had guided her life for nearly thirty years, and it hadn't been as bad as she'd expected. The world hadn't imploded, and she hadn't ended up heartbroken. At least, not yet. She handed Nick a glass of wine. "Where do we start?"

"Here," he said, then kissed her again. This time, he lingered, his kiss deep and true and tasting of chardonnay. She curved into his arms, arching into his chest, wanting more, wanting him, wanting whatever this was. In the background, Bing gave way to Burl Ives's peppier "Holly Jolly Christmas."

Nick stepped back. "We're never going to get this tree decorated if we keep doing that."

"Nothing wrong with a naked tree."

He laughed. "I do like your train of thought, Viv. But let's at least get some lights on there. Ellie will love that."

A part of her heart melted at the thoughtfulness in Nick's words. The tree, the lights, were about making a three-month-old happy. A baby who would never remember this moment, or this tree. Nevertheless, Nick had slipped fully into the role of surrogate father—protective, considerate and sweet.

Those were good qualities in a man. The kind of qualities a smart woman hung on to and treasured. Except some smart women had careers in another city, and lives too cramped to have room for a child and a husband. Some smart women had never dared to dream of a man like Nick.

As she crossed to the decorations box, she saw the other box with Nick's name on the outside, still sitting in the corner. "What's that?"

"A request." Nick sighed and dropped into the armchair. "My grandmother left it for me to give to my father. She actually listed it in her will as a condition of me receiving my inheritance. She wants us to go through the box together. Why, I have no idea. I looked in there, and it's just a bunch of stuff from his childhood."

"The same father who doesn't talk to you?" Vivian sat on the ottoman across from him.

Nick nodded. "I called him and told him about it, and his words were, 'drop it in the mail.' Even this final request from his mother wasn't worth him coming around to see his own son."

"His name sounds familiar. I'm sure he is doing all that because he's probably a very stubborn man." She paused, thinking of the lawyers she knew, the ones who would argue to the death for a small point, the ones who had been divorced many times or were on the outs with their families. Time and again, she'd seen the same common thread. "Or a very hurt one."

"What makes you say that?"

As the words coalesced in Vivian's mind, she saw the connections, the echoes between her childhood and Nick's. Perhaps that was what had brought them together, these shared wounds. "My mom hardly visited Sammie and I when we were placed in foster care. She messed up so many times that I stopped counting on her, although it took Sammie a lot longer to do that.

When I was fifteen or sixteen, Sammie and I waited all afternoon at a playground for her to show up. Sammie was only eleven or so, and still so optimistic and sure that our mother would be there. She'd worn her best dress, and had our foster mother braid her hair. She'd drawn a picture of the three of us to give to Mom when we saw her."

"And she didn't show up?"

"She did. Two hours late. By then, Sammie's dress was dirty, her braids were loose and the picture was crinkled." Vivian shook her head. She could still see the defeat in Sammie's eyes, the tears that trickled through the dirt on her cheeks. "Then I saw my mom, standing at the edge of the park and marched over to her. I read her the riot act for five minutes straight."

Nick smiled. "That I can imagine you doing."

"My argument skills have always been pretty strong." Vivian took a sip of wine, and in her mind she was that teenager again, trying to put all those hurts from her childhood together, and drag answers out of the one person who had never given her any. "I asked her why she even bothered to set up visitations if all she was going to do was bail at the last minute. And she said…"

When Vivian didn't continue, Nick reached out and touched her hand. "She said what?"

"That she felt so guilty about being such a bad mom that she couldn't bring herself to face us. She knew she'd screwed up. Knew she'd said things and done things that had hurt us, and it was easier for her to ignore us than to apologize. Or show up and deal with how much she had let us down." Vivian leaned to-ward Nick. "Some people just don't know how to deal with the pain they've caused. Maybe your dad is one of them."

"Maybe. Or maybe he's just a stubborn man who can't admit he's wrong."

"Kinda the same thing, don't you think?" Vivian gave him a soft smile.

"You may be right." He got to his feet and pulled an extension cord from one of the boxes. "Do you think that's part of why your sister has stayed away? She knows she let you and Ellie down and she can't face that right now?"

Vivian thought of the conversation with Della, the challenges of being a new mom and the sense of fail-ure when things went awry. "Maybe."

The heavy conversation was making Vivian far too self-reflective. Her mind pulled at threads of her own avoidance of relationships and connections. But that was a knot she was nowhere near ready to untangle. She'd much rather be hanging plastic Santas on the tree. "Well, let's get this tree decorated before it gets too late." Vivian dug in the box marked Decorations, and pulled out two strings of multicolored lights. "I hope they still work."

"They do. I tested them the other day." Nick started at the top, wrapping the tree with the lights, weav-ing them in and out of the branches, then adding the second string and a third that she discovered under a container of ornaments. "Turn off the lights," he said.

"Why?"

"Because the first time we light this tree, I want to get the full effect."

She did as he requested, and the room plunged into darkness. "Silent Night" began to play on the radio. A second later, Nick had plugged in the lights, and a bloom of red, green, blue and yellow filled the living room. The soft strains of the Christmas carol made the room feel hushed, almost sacred.

Nick came to stand beside her. "It's beautiful."

"It is." Vivian had seen hundreds of Christmas trees over the years—mostly on TV or in magazine ads—but none seemed as precious as this tilted, barely decorated one. Maybe because she'd chosen the tree, this part of the family as Cutler had called it. She turned to Nick. "This is going to sound crazy, but one of the things I've always wanted to do is lie under a Christmas tree and look up at the lights."

He considered her for a moment, a quirk of amusement in his features. "I don't think it's crazy at all. Let's do it."

Like two ten-year-olds, they lay on their backs and shimmied under the tree. Their heads pressed together, and a dusting of needles scattered across their faces and chests. Vivian giggled. Actually giggled. She couldn't remember the last time she'd done that, if ever. Above her head, the lights blinked on-off, on-off, a constellation of colors nestled among the branches. "It's like fireworks. So cool."

"It is." Nick's hand covered hers. They lay there for a while, silent, while Christmas carols played in the background and the lights twinkled.

Nick kept holding her hand. He was close enough that she could feel the warmth from his body, inhale the scent of his cologne. She could get used to this. Very used to it.

At the same time, they turned to look at each other. Neither said a word, but their hands tightened and they drew closer. Nick cupped her face, then kissed her, and before she knew it, she was pressed up against him and he was devouring her, and Vivian Winthrop finally stopped overthinking the whole thing.

Chapter Eleven

Nick had told himself—very firmly and many, many times—that he was not going to do anything more than kiss Vivian. Then she'd worn that dress, and his resolve had melted a little. But what tipped the scales from no to yes had been that moment under the tree when she'd turned to him, the look in her eyes both sultry and vulnerable, and all those arguments in his head disappeared. Whatever reservations he'd had about Vivian vanished in light of that vulnerable conversation and that moment under the tree.

He took her hand, pulled her to her feet. She swayed into his arms. "What are we doing?" he asked, repeating her question from earlier.

"I don't know. I just know..." Her blue eyes met his, and in them, a dark storm brewed. "I don't want to stop."

"Neither do I." His voice was a hoarse rasp. Blood raced through his veins, thudded in his heart. Her hair had come undone, and the combination of the loose tangles and the sexiness of her bare shoulders nearly undid him. "I want to take you up to my room and—"

"Then do it, Nick. Please."

It was the *please* that erased the last of his resistance. He'd wanted Vivian almost from the second he met her, but she'd made it clear she wasn't a long-term girl. Maybe he was blind or a fool, but all he saw when he looked at her was long-term. She had committed to her sister, to her career, and in a fierce, deep way that he admired. She had passion, and he wanted to explore every inch of that.

He took her hand and they went upstairs, passing the nursery where Ellie still slept, and turning left to Nick's room, at the end of the hall. He started to shut the door, then left it slightly ajar. "Just in case Ellie wakes up."

"And that," she said, tangling her hands in his hair, "is why I want you."

"Because I'm leaving the door open?"

"Because you are thoughtful…" She pressed a kiss to his neck. "Considerate…" Another kiss. "Kind…" A third. "And gentle."

The desire that had simmered all day inside him flamed into an overpowering need. It was all he could do to stand still, while she kissed and teased him. "Is that what you want me to be, Vivian? Gentle?"

She drew back and met his gaze head-on. "I want

you to love me, Nick. Just for tonight. We'll worry about gentle later."

Good Lord. Did this woman know what she did to him when she said things like that? He scooped her up and laid her on the bed, then kicked off his shoes. She started to do the same, but he put a hand on her bare leg. "Leave the heels on. Please."

Her brows arched. A devilish smile lit her face. "My, my, Nick Jackson. You do surprise me."

"Good." He undid his shirt and tie, tossing them to the side. "Because you're the kind of woman who deserves to be surprised. And loved. No, not just loved, but loved well."

He climbed onto the bed beside her. She rolled toward him, and he reached for the zipper on the back of her dress, then stopped. Tears shimmered in her eyes. "Did I say something wrong? Did you change your mind?"

"No. Not at all." She cupped his face and kissed him. "I want you more than I've ever wanted anyone and…it scares me."

"To want something you can lose?"

"Something I *will* say goodbye to." She let out a long breath. "I don't want to give you a forever impression, Nick. Let's just have tonight, and tomorrow will sort itself out."

Something I will say goodbye to.

When he heard the words, he realized how much he'd hoped Vivian would stay in Stone Gap. That this little temporary family could become permanent and real. The truth was, none of this was real. Ellie wasn't theirs, they weren't each other's, and very soon their lives would diverge in two radically different directions.

He would have tonight, and that would be it. Would that be enough?

For the first time in his life, Nick was afraid, too, of losing someone he'd begun to care very deeply about. It had taken Ariel walking out of his life for him to see how shallow his feelings for her had been. Losing her had smarted, of course, but only for few weeks. But the thought of never seeing Vivian again—

If he thought about it long enough, it would damned near make him stop breathing.

"Tonight, Nick. Let's just pretend," she said. Then she kissed him again, curving against him as she did, her hands roving over his bare back, lingering along his waistband, and Nick stopped thinking. The zipper on the back of Vivian's dress slid down with a soft snick, and a second later, she'd kicked it to the floor.

"Damn, you're beautiful." He kissed a trail from her jaw to the valley between her breasts, then over the cleavage that spilled out of the black strapless bra. She shifted up on the bed as he kept moving down, kissing, licking, teasing. He tugged off her panties, then slid between her legs.

The easy softness in her disappeared, and her body stiffened. "I've, uh…never…"

He shifted back to lie beside her again. He danced an easy caress across her belly. "I'm not going to lie, that makes me pretty damned happy to hear."

"I just don't know if I can…" Her cheeks flushed,

"well, you know. I don't want you to feel like you're doing something wrong if I don't…get there. I don't usually in general. Most of the guys I've been with have been kind of…fast and well… Anyway, I don't want you to be disappointed."

He cupped her face. "Vivian, *nothing* about you disappoints me. You are strong and fierce and gorgeous. And any man who didn't appreciate that, appreciate every inch of you, is the wrong man to be with."

That adorable blush appeared in her cheeks again, then she danced a tentative hand down his pants to cup him. The sensation of her soft, warm hand against him instantly made him even harder. The desire raging inside him urged to take her, hard and fast, but tonight, it was all about making Vivian feel good. "As much as I want you to do that forever," he said, "I think it's your turn."

She nodded, then smiled as he kissed his way down her breasts, across her belly and back to her legs. She laid back, propping her feet on the bed, the black spiked heels digging into the comforter while he tasted her. He went slow at first, teasing her, dancing around the outer edges, before coming back to the center.

She moaned, writhing against his tongue. Her hands tangled in his hair, and when he moved deeper, faster, and harder, she gasped, arched against the bed, and a moment later, shouted his name. "Oh my…that was… unbelievable."

He grinned, and slid back up her body. "Well, let's see if we can make you do that again. And again."

That devilish look flashed in her eyes again. "You think you're up to the challenge?"

"I'll take whatever challenge you throw at me, Vivian." And when he finally slipped inside Vivian's body, he made sure to appreciate her very, very much. She was fiery and sweet, passionate and tender.

And somewhere along the way between the gazebo and the bedroom, Nick Jackson fell head over heels in love.

The sun had just started to crest when Vivian opened her eyes. Nick's chest rose and fell in steady, even breaths. She had her head on the valley beneath his shoulder, her hand on his abdomen and one leg wrapped around his body.

She moved back, out from under his arm, as carefully and quietly as she could. What had she been thinking? Making love with him—and yes, holy hell, that had been amazing, both the first and the second time—and then sleeping beside him? She never spent the night with men. Never let them stay at her place. That kind of thing led to too many misconceptions about what she could offer them.

It had been sex, plain and simple. Just sex.

Right?

Even in sleep, Nick had a hint of a smile on his face. She sat back on her knees and watched him for a moment. He was a handsome man, with a chiseled jaw and one lock of hair that often fell across his brows. He clearly worked out—given the muscular planes of his chest and abs. But it was the heart of the man that she was most attracted to. The man she had slept beside, and the man she knew she should leave.

When she thought of last night, of his tenderness and consideration, her resolve softened. Nick had done more than just make her orgasm—he had shown her there were men who cared enough to put her needs first. All her life, she had avoided long-term relationships—and not once had she ever regretted it or even had a second thought. Maybe she'd chosen poorly, but most of the men she'd dated had been selfish and emotionally closed off. Not Nick. He wore his emotions on his chef's apron, and was as open as a prairie.

That was dangerous. Because it was the kind of thing she could fall for.

Or maybe already had. Something about him had her seriously considering staying in Stone Gap. Staying meant going all in with what he wanted—a family, a forever. Despite her speech about her mother that night, a part of Vivian had always been afraid that she would turn out to be just as bad of a mother. Emotionally unavailable to her husband, her children, and basically addicted to work, instead of her family. Work was her comfort zone, the one place where she felt sure and confident.

She started to slip off the bed when Nick stirred. "Hey, don't get up yet. Ellie's still sleeping." He patted the mattress beside him. "Come back to bed with me."

The thick white comforter and soft sheets beckoned her. She could easily slide back into that bed with Nick and pretend, just a little longer, that this was her life. Her man. Her family.

Outside the window, the Saturday-morning sun continued ascending. Yesterday she'd called her contractor and made sure the apartment was near enough to done to be habitable. Which meant tomorrow, she would go home to Durham with Ellie, then hire someone to take care of the baby for the hours after the day care closed. And all of this, whatever this was, with Nick would be over. That was for the best. Before she hurt him, or disappointed him too.

"You sleep in. I have some work to do," she said, then hurried out of the room before she changed her mind.

She took a quick shower, dressed in jeans and a T-shirt, then settled in at the dining room table with her laptop and a stack of files and briefs to read. She could hear Ellie beginning to stir, and the patter of Nick's feet as he headed into the nursery.

"Good morning, sunshine," he said to Ellie, the words happy and sweet, and just the kind of words every little girl should hear when she woke up. "You hungry?"

The words on the page in front of Vivian swam. She closed her eyes and pinched the bridge of her nose, but when she opened her eyes again, everything was a teary blur. Did she really have to leave this weekend? Couldn't she wrangle a few more days in Stone Gap?

She got to her feet and was halfway down the hall to go talk to him when the doorbell rang. At six thirty in the morning? Who on earth would be coming by that early? Vivian pulled open the door to find Sammie standing on the doorstep, wearing the same jeans and T-shirt she'd been wearing the day she left, with a backpack slung over one shoulder and a brand-new stuffed white bear under her other arm.

"Hi, Viv! I'm back!" Sammie grinned. Her sister looked healthy and happy, better than she'd looked in years. Maybe the time on her own had been a good thing after all. "The people at the inn told me where you were staying. For a second, I thought you'd left town. Where's my little girl? I can't wait to hold her again."

Vivian glanced up the staircase and saw Nick, holding Ellie, with her favorite pink bunny blanket clutched between them. An unreadable expression filled his face. In that instant, Vivian realized that once again, her world had imploded. But this time, the implosion would be affecting Nick and Ellie, too.

"She just got up," Nick said.

Sammie's gaze shot to Nick. As soon as she spied the baby, Sammie barreled up the stairs, her arms out and reaching for her daughter. "Ellie! Oh my God, I've missed you so much!"

Nick glanced at Vivian. She gave him a small nod of assent, and he handed Ellie over to her mother. Sammie drew the baby tight to her chest, covering her with kisses, talking nonstop. The bear squished between them. Ellie stared at Sammie, but didn't cry. "You got so big! I swear, you've gained five pounds. Oh, Momma has been so sad without her Ellie girl."

"I was just about to change her," Nick said to Sammie. He still had his hands halfway between them, ready to take the baby back at any second. "Do you want me to—"

"I can do it. Then I can spend time with my little Ellie Boo." Sammie nuzzled Ellie's stomach which made Ellie let out a little giggle, then turned into the nursery. She kept on talking to Ellie as she changed her.

Nick came down the stairs, his steps heavy and slow. Vivian waited in the foyer, her heart a riot of mixed emotions. Joy, loss, regret, sadness. "She's back," she said to Nick. "For Ellie."

Gratitude for Sammie's safe return was quickly chased by frustration with the entire chain of events. Sammie had just walked out, assuming Vivian would take care of everything for her, like she always did. If Vivian hadn't been here, what would have happened to Ellie? And now, Sammie expected to waltz back into their lives as if nothing happened? How did Vivian know for sure that Sammie wouldn't do this again? There wasn't going to be a Nick standing in the kitchen the next time.

"I'm sure that's best," Nick said, but his words were edged with concern. "Ellie should be with her mother. Not her aunt and a...stranger, or whatever I am...or was." He shook his head and let out a little cough. For a second, he stared at the hardwood floor, looking lost and distracted. "Since you don't need me here, I, uh, should probably get to the inn. It's almost time for breakfast. Will you be by today?"

"Actually..." Now was as good a time as any to tell him her plans. If there was one thing Vivian had learned in law, it was that dealing with the facts was a lot easier once they were all on the table. She had no reason to delay her departure, now that Sammie had returned. And maybe it would be easier if she just told Nick now, while her heart was already hurting. "I'm going to go back to Durham today."

He wheeled back to her. "What? Now?"

"I was going to go tomorrow but now that Sammie's here, I don't have any reason to stay." Nick winced, and Vivian wished she could take the words back. "I meant, I have a job—"

"I know what you meant." He scowled. "By all means, run back to Durham."

"I'm not running. I have a court case and work, and that renovation to oversee—"

"And what about us?" Even though Sammie was still in the nursery with Ellie, Nick lowered his voice.

Vivian raised her chin. "What about it? We had a great time, and made some memories. And got a Christmas tree. I call that a successful evening."

He scoffed. "A successful *evening*? Is that code for—" he lowered his voice even more "'—thanks for the sex, Nick, I'll send you a postcard once in a while'?"

The harsh words made her recoil. Last night had been wonderful, yes, so why couldn't Nick understand that one night, one date, would have to be enough? That even if she wanted to try to take this further, she also knew that they didn't have what it took to make this anything more? Or rather, that she didn't? The last thing she wanted to do was make him think she could be that family woman he kept seeing her as. "That wasn't what that was, and you know it."

"Oh yeah? Then what was it? For you? Because it was a lot more than one night for me," he said, as if he'd just read her mind. Nick took a step closer to her, placing one hand on her waist. She wanted to lean into the warmth of his hand, into him, into this. "I want you, Vivian. Not for one night. Forever."

Forever. The word alternately terrified and thrilled her. Nick wanted something permanent. Pretty ironic that the very thing she'd always craved was right before her, and she was throwing it aside. But she knew that life wasn't for her. And trying to make it work would only hurt them both even more in the long run.

"I'm not a forever kind of girl, Nick," she said. "I'll just let you down in the end. You should know that by now."

"Honey, you have forever written all over you. The problem is, you're too damned scared to take it when it's right in front of you. You're like your mother, standing at the edge of the playground, afraid to go in and visit with your daughters. Take the leap, Vivian."

Damn it. Why did he keep calling her *honey*? It was all she could do not to kiss him right there. An insane thought because she was in the middle of telling him they were done. "It's not that. I can't just up and leave my job. You make it sound like I can settle down here and be your sous chef or something."

"I never said that. You want to live in Durham? Fine, we'll live in Durham. You want to live here? We'll live here. They need chefs pretty much everywhere in the world, so I'm good with wherever you need to be. What's more important to me, Vivian, than where I work, is who I come home to. And that I have a home. Not just a room in the back of a B and B."

Or an apartment in Durham as sterile as a hospital room. Ida Mae's house, with all its memories and mementos, felt more like home than any place Vivian had ever lived. The tree in the corner, its lights muted for now, was hers. Well, hers and Nick's. They'd bought it, set it in the stand, hung it with lights. Turned this place into a home in just a few days.

He wanted to build a home with her. Come home to her. Make something that would last, beyond this week and this holiday season. She should have been elated, should have leaped into his arms and said yes, yes, yes. Instead, fear tightened her chest and shortened her breath, and she backed away from him.

"I can't do that, Nick. I'm sorry." She tore her gaze away from his because if she looked at the hurt in his eyes one more time, she'd lose her resolve. "I'm just going to see if Sammie needs anything, and then I'll start packing. Say goodbye to Della and Mavis for me, will you?"

She headed upstairs. Even as she loaded her clothes into her suitcase and her files into her briefcase, she couldn't shake the feeling that she was leaving something very important behind.

Chapter Twelve

After the breakfast shift, Nick mixed up a quick chicken salad for the guests for lunch, adding a bowl of washed fruit and a hearty potato salad he'd made the day before. Once the food was laid out and the beef stew he'd made for dinner was simmering, Nick stood in the kitchen, with nothing to do, and knew he'd put the decision off long enough.

Vivian was leaving. Sammie had Ellie. The little charade of a life they'd been living had come to an end. And that meant Nick had no excuse to keep him from the conversation he'd been dreading for months.

"Mavis, I'll be back this afternoon." He hung his apron on the hook by the pantry, grabbed his keys from the shelf by the door, then headed out to his truck.

When he got inside, he noticed a forgotten pacifier from Ellie on the backseat.

Damn.

Nick turned it over in his hand. His chest ached, and damned if he wasn't half close to tears for a kid that wasn't even his. Maybe it wasn't the baby so much as the potential she had awakened in him. A dream of a forever with Vivian and him. A child of their own someday. More nights on the couch and dances in the gazebo.

Bah humbug. Nick tossed the pacifier into the glove box, put the truck in gear, then headed back to Ida Mae's. His grandmother's house echoed with emptiness. Sammie had taken Ellie with her. Where they'd gone, Nick had no idea. Rather than sticking around to ask, he had ducked out of there as soon as Vivian said she was leaving.

Vivian's car was gone, and so was her suitcase. The dining room table held no files, the bathroom held no makeup. All that was left was a crib and diaper bag in a nursery that would never be used again.

Nick picked up the box he'd pulled out of the attic last week and set it on the kitchen table. Then he picked up his cell phone and dialed his father's number. It took four rings before Richard answered. Had he been standing there, debating whether to pick up?

"Nicholas. What did you need?"

Nick sighed. "I know you're in Stone Gap today. Thought you might want to come by and get the box Grandma left for you."

"You can drop it off at my office. I'm about to head back there."

Nick bit back his first, instinctive response. And his second. He thought of Vivian's words, about how his father's distance was more about fear than disappointment. He found that hard to equate with the cold man who had raised him.

Had his father held Nick when he was an infant and marveled at his fingers and toes? Laughed when his tiny hand gripped one finger? Paced the halls when Nick's cries wouldn't stop? Had he ever, for a second, loved his sons the way Nick had begun to love Ellie?

"It's Christmas, Dad. Can we just pretend we're a family for a couple hours? Swing by Grandma's and I'll give you the box in person, like she wanted." There was more to his grandmother's request, but Nick kept it simple for now. His father would be less likely to come if he knew it would be more complicated than just accepting the box.

Like his father had said, Grandma wouldn't know if Nick didn't abide by every part of her letter, which had asked him to sit with his father and go through the contents. Except, Nick would know. And he owed the woman who had been more of a parent than anyone in his life this one last request.

His father sighed. "I have a meeting—"

"Screw the meeting. You have a son who wants to see you, and I think that takes precedence, don't you?"

A long pause. A sigh. "I'll be there in ten minutes."

"See you then." But the phone call had already ended and Nick was talking to the air.

His father pulled into the driveway fifteen minutes later. He locked the Mercedes with a double beep, then climbed the stairs. Nick pulled open the door before Richard knocked. "I have to say, I'm surprised you came."

Richard scowled. "It was out of my way."

Good to see his father was his regular warm and cuddly self. "Come on in."

His father entered the house and paused in the foyer. His gaze went to the Christmas tree, the decorations. For a moment, his features were unreadable, then he cleared his throat and strode into the kitchen. Nick had left Ida Mae's letter on the table beside the box. His father began to reach for the box.

"I think you need to read the letter first," Nick said.

His father shot him a look of annoyance, but sat down at the table to read the letter. It was short, just a single sheet of paper, but Richard seemed to take forever to read it. When he put the letter back on the table, his hand shook. "She always did see me with different eyes than I saw myself with."

"Grandma was good at that. She saw the best in everyone she met."

"I've always been more like my father. He was a loner. Hardly ever showed any emotion unless he was with my mother. He was a stoic man, but a marshmallow with her." Richard cleared his throat. "I see you, uh, decorated the house."

"Yeah. I wanted one more holiday here." Nick left out the rest, because it was far too painful to tell anyone that the holiday he'd dreamed of had walked out the door a few hours ago.

"It looks like it did when I was a kid. That's nice, Nicholas." His father fiddled with the letter. "Your grandmother said she wants us to go through the box together."

"Yeah. I have no idea why."

"I think I do." Richard pulled open the lid, then took out the first few things and set them on the table, talking as he did. "She wanted me to remember what I used to be like. When I was a kid, I was more like you than Grady or Carson."

Nick scoffed. "I find that hard to believe."

"This glove," his father said, "was pretty much welded onto my hand most of my childhood. I played on every Little League team I could find. I thought someday I'd end up in the major leagues. Me and Matty."

Nick had forgotten that his father had grown up with Matty Gibson, the owner of the grocery store downtown. "He did go on to the major leagues, didn't he?"

His father nodded. "He got signed by the Braves but barely started the season. Tore his rotator cuff, he ended up coming back here, taking over his father's market, and never living his dream again." His father reached in the box and pulled out the autograph book. "My dad would take me to ball games sometimes. I'd wait outside the stadium afterward and get the players to sign my book. I told them all I'd grow up to be like them someday."

Nick couldn't imagine his suit-wearing, stern father as a kid, sitting outside a baseball stadium, an eager fan seeing his heroes. "But you went into law instead."

"Yeah." His father sighed. He pushed the box aside and picked up the letter again. "My mother, God bless her, thought she was doing the right thing."

"What do you mean?"

"My dad died when I was seventeen. I had a chance that summer to play for a travel team, sort of a year-round thing for the best players. Matty was going, and I'd been selected to be the shortstop. Everyone knew that college and major league scouts came by to watch this particular team because they only picked kids who'd had pretty knockout high school careers. That's how Matty ended up getting signed later. A scout saw him, and offered him a major league position. Matty's dad insisted he get a couple years of college first, but then he went to the big leagues."

"And you didn't."

"I didn't because I didn't go with the team. I turned down the opportunity." His father let out a long breath. "I haven't thought about any of this in a long damned time. And didn't want to. But after you called the other day, I started wondering what my mother could possibly have held onto all these years and I realized it had to be my baseball stuff. I guess this is her way of apologizing."

"Apologizing? For what?" The grandmother he remembered had been kind and loving, and probably the best person Nick had ever met.

"For talking me out of going with the team. I stayed

home that summer to help my mother. She was a wreck after my dad died. She could barely function. To help make ends meet, I went to work in a law office, as a gofer of sorts, and she told me I should bet on the sure thing and let the rest go. So I did."

Nick thought of his own career. How he'd worked for so long in a career he hated because it was a sure thing. If his life hadn't imploded, he never would have come here and taken the chef job. Security. It was what Sammie had been seeking for her daughter, what Vivian retreated to whenever she got scared and what he had banked on for a lot of unhappy years.

"I watched Matty's career take off as the years passed, and I was angry. Resentful. Jealous. I blamed my mom for my choice to give up the career I wanted, so I guess I thought I was punishing her by staying away and being the most successful lawyer I could be. Turns out—" his father let out a long breath "—I was punishing myself. I could barely stand in that funeral home that day. I felt like such a terrible son for not being here. For her. For you."

Vivian had been right. His father had been overcome by his regrets, and so sure he couldn't earn forgiveness. Richard had been harsh and cold to his boys—there was no disputing that—but he had also been a man in pain for a long, long time. A man who could argue for hours in a courtroom but couldn't bring himself to say anything that came from his heart.

"I didn't stop talking to you because I hated you, Nick. None of that crap I said about you being a disappointment was true. I stopped talking because…" His stoic, pressed, severe father's face began to crumple. "I didn't know how to say what I needed to say. That I was envious that you took the risks I was afraid to take. That you went after what you wanted, what you were passionate about. While I sat in my office day after day, making a paycheck and counting my regrets."

The kitchen clocked ticked past the hour. A tree rattled against the windows. The scent of the glove oil hung in the air. Here was the moment Nick had wanted. A chance to tell his father what he thought of all those years of silence. The missed father-son opportunities. The resentments that had built and built.

Instead, Nick opened his heart and let all that go. What was the point, really? They'd each made their own mistakes to get to this point.

Nick reached in the box and pulled out a worn baseball, the leather cover grayed by age and years of use. It sat smooth and heavy in his palm. He tossed it up and down a couple times. "Dad, now that you're here, why don't you finally teach me how to catch?"

Richard got to his feet, grabbed Nick and hauled his son to his chest. The two of them stood there for a long, long time. Then they went into the yard and tossed the ball back and forth until the sun began to go down. Anyone going by wouldn't have seen two grown men working out decades of issues. They'd have heard and seen exactly what it was—a father and son bonding.

The day before Christmas, Vivian sat in the conference room at the office and faced the man who she had taken on pro bono almost a year ago. She'd been home for two weeks and poured herself into her work, sometimes sleeping at the office. Winter was definitely in the North Carolina air, and most of her office had already left for the holidays.

But here she was, on a Sunday, working, as she had last Sunday and all the ones before that. Ellie sat in her car seat beside Vivian's chair, content and recently fed. When she stirred, Vivian reached in and picked her up. The baby sat on Vivian's lap and watched her tiny hands press into the wood table. Sammie was supposed to drop by soon, to pick up Ellie on her way home from work and give Vivian some time to stay late at work.

Ellie had become a frequent companion at the office. Vivian couldn't spend all day here with the baby because it threw Ellie off her schedule, but a couple hours a day worked out pretty well and meshed with Sammie's flexible waitressing schedule. Still, a part of Vivian ached every time she saw her niece. Sammie had her life together now, more or less. She had found a better paying job, but was still struggling financially, so Vivian had offered to let her and Ellie move in with her now that the apartment renovations had been completed. For the first time since Vivian had moved into the building, the apartment felt like a home. Not because of the new granite countertops or hardwood floors, but because of the stuffed animals on the floor and baby bottles in the sink. At the same time, every one of those things reminded Vivian of Nick. She found her mind wandering during the day, pondering what he was doing.

The hole in Vivian's life only widened when day after day went by without a word from Nick. A part of her had thought he'd chase after her in some grand romantic gesture. But there'd been nothing, not a word. Maybe he'd accepted the same facts that she had— they wanted different lives. Or maybe her bailing on him had made him give up.

Jerry sat at the huge mahogany table, flanked by his wife, who gave Ellie a little wave and a smile. The papers Vivian had drawn up sat in front of the couple. Legally, she was compelled to present the settlement offer to her client, even if she thought it was a paltry sum that was far less than he deserved. For a long moment, no one said a word.

"This is quite a sizable offer," Jerry said. His right arm rested on the table, a little smaller and weaker than his left. Long steel rods had replaced the shattered bones, and months of physical therapy had brought him back to 80 percent. He'd never be 100 percent again, and never go back to his assembly job. "It will help out a lot. And they offered an apology and are recalling the rest of those machines."

"I think we can fight for more," Vivian said. "I have enough documentation here to prove that this equipment manufacturer has a long list of shop violations, and shoddy workmanship with their machinery. You won't be able to work the same job again, and you still have years of therapy ahead of you. For all that, you deserve at least three times that in compensation."

"How long will a lawsuit like that take?"

"If they refuse to make a new offer and insist on a trial, it could be three, four years. Unfortunately, these kinds of cases drag out. The lawyers for the other side will file everything they can, and ask for extensions at every step of the process. They want to drag it out so that hopefully you'll give up. But I'm here to fight for all of you. I know what this has done to your family and your life." She nodded toward Jerry. "You've lost your home and your car, and had to depend on your family members for charity when you were out of work for six months, recuperating. But if you can just hold on a little—"

"No." Jerry glanced at his wife. She took his hand and gave him a slight nod. "Me and the wife, we talked this morning. And we decided that no matter what the offer was, we were going to take it."

"But you could have so much more—"

"No offense, Ms. Winthrop, but I don't think you know what it's like to get up in the morning and look in your wife's eyes or your kids' and see their fear and disappointment because you lost their home. It takes a toll on a man, on a family. This might not be as much money as we could have if we held out, but the wife and I don't care about that. This will be enough money to pay the medical bills and get us back on our feet and under our own roof." He pulled out a pen and clicked the top.

"Wait, before you sign." Vivian bounced Ellie on her lap. The baby clutched at Vivian's shirt. "Is there nothing I can do to convince you to pursue this further? I have a strong case and no doubt that we will prevail."

"We appreciate how hard you've worked on this, but you gotta understand something." Jerry cleared his throat. "The morning after we lost our home, I woke up in the basement of my cousin's house, all four of us cramped in one sofa bed, with our belongings stacked up around us like a wall. I spent fifteen years saving for the down payment on that house, another five years fixing it up and making it into the kind of place where Marie and I could raise our kids. And just like that, it was gone. I should have been depressed. Should have been mad as hell, or something. But instead, I was… and you're going to think I'm crazy for saying this, but I was happy."

Vivian stared at him. This man, who had undergone three surgeries, months of painful rehabilitation and suffered devastating losses had been happy? "How is that possible after all you and your family went through?"

"I had what mattered with me. My wife under my arm, my son under the other arm and our fierce and stubborn little girl sleeping on the end of the bed." Jerry chuckled. "She's the kind of kid who goes left when you say right. Drives me crazy, but I wouldn't trade her for all the kids in the world. Anyway, I looked at all of them, and yes, I felt like I had let them down, but I was also grateful as hell to have the only thing that would break me if I lost it—my family. This is enough money to let me take care of them the way I should—to get our lives back on track, and for me, that's good enough."

"I'm…surprised. I don't think I've ever had a client who said they didn't want to fight for more money." She was used to being the lawyer who dug in her heels, who fought—and won—against impossible odds.

"It's Christmas," Jerry said. "I just want to go home and enjoy the holiday and hug my kids." His wife nodded. "And I'm sure you'd rather be anywhere but in this office this time of year, especially since it's that little one's first holiday. So go home and enjoy the people you love. We're very grateful to you for taking on our case, Ms. Winthrop. But if it's okay with you, I'm just going to sign this and go. I promised the kids I'd help decorate the tree tonight." He swooped his signature across the settlement offer, then slid the paper across the table.

Vivian stared at them both, stunned. "When I met you that night, you were so broke, Jerry. All I wanted to do was change your life."

"You did." Jerry smiled. "And what's better, because those machines are being recalled, you're saving other people the pain we went through. I'd say that's enough of a Christmas present for everyone." He rose and handed her the document. "Go home to your family, Ms. Winthrop. Me and mine will be just fine. Merry Christmas."

Nick stood in the glass-and-marble foyer, and wondered if he was a fool. He'd shown up here without calling, without texting, without even checking to see if Vivian would talk to him. It was a crazy idea.

He'd spent two miserable weeks in Stone Gap, a misery compounded by several meals at the inn going awry because Nick's mind was here in Durham, and not in the kitchen. It got so bad that Mavis pulled him aside and told him to *either go get that girl, or go back to culinary school*.

So here he was, on Christmas Eve, in the lobby of the towering building that housed the Veritas Law firm. He'd taken a chance coming here on a weekend before a holiday. He almost turned around, then saw Vivian's car in the parking lot. Only a handful of cars sat in the lot, which made hers stick out even more. He wasn't surprised to find her here, even on Christmas Eve.

He scanned the sign mounted beside the elevator. Veritas Law took up four floors in the building. No indication of which floor held Vivian's office. He picked a number at random and pushed the button. The screen above the car counted down the elevator's approach to the lobby: 12, 11, 10.

A few seconds later, the elevator dinged and the doors opened. Nick moved forward, putting out a hand to stop the doors from closing. As he did, Vivian stepped out and into the foyer. For a solid five seconds, he couldn't think. She was holding Ellie against her chest and had a diaper bag over one shoulder. "Nick. What are you doing here?"

"Looking for you." Now that Vivian was standing before him, all those pretty words he'd composed in his head on the trip up here disappeared. Damn, she looked good. A dark blue dress hugged her curves. Black heels showed off those incredible legs. The long hair he loved was pinned up. And Ellie—she looked like she'd grown three inches. Her big blue eyes stared at him and as recognition dawned, they lit up and she reached for him.

"Seems like she remembers you." Vivian laughed, gave Ellie a kiss on her cheek, then handed the baby to Nick in one fluid movement. Vivian's ease with the baby surprised him almost as much as finding her behind the elevator doors.

"Did Sammie leave again?" Nick gave Ellie a grin, then nuzzled her cheek. In answer, she grabbed his shirt. Damn, she smelled of freshness and hope, and he hadn't realized until just now how much he'd missed this little booger.

"No. She'll be here in a minute to get Ellie. She's just getting off work now."

As if on cue, there was a beep behind him. He turned and watched Sammie pull into the lot and park her beat-up Toyota. Vivian headed out to the lot and greeted her sister with a hug. Nick trailed along behind, surprised as hell. "I just fed her. But I think her diaper will need to be changed," Vivian said. "I think she's teething so don't forget to put the teething ring in the freezer for a few minutes."

Nick stared at Vivian as if she was speaking a foreign language.

"Thanks." Sammie turned to Nick. Vivian's sister

looked happier and brighter than the last time he'd seen her. "Hi, Nick."

"Hi, Sammie." He didn't know what else to do or say so he handed Ellie over. His arms felt too empty already. "Uh, Merry Christmas."

Sammie just grinned. She slipped the diaper bag off Vivian's arm and onto her own. "Did you tell him yet?"

"No."

"Okay. Well, I'll meet you there. See you soon, Nick!" Sammie grinned again, then turned on her heel and hurried to her car. A few minutes later, she was gone.

Meet her there? See him soon?

"What was that about?" Nick asked.

"Nothing." A breeze kicked up, scattering leaves across the tarred lot. Vivian drew her coat tighter.

He swallowed his disappointment. What had he expected? That she'd jump into his arms and they'd have some kind of Nicholas Sparks ending? He'd shown up unannounced, without much of a plan. "I was hoping we could talk."

"Okay," she said. "I know it's a little chilly out, but what do you say to a walk?"

Considering how much he'd moped around the rooms at the inn, being outside would probably do him some good. Although half of him was convinced she was just going to tell him to give up already. "Sure."

When she slipped into place beside him, the scent of her perfume teased him. Reminded him of that single night they'd shared. Damn. What kind of glutton for punishment was he, anyway?

"Are you sure you want to walk?" he asked. "You have on heels."

"Where I want to go isn't very far away." She reached for his hand, and led him through the parking lot to a paved path that circled the back of the building.

Okay, so she was holding his hand. He'd take that as a good sign. A sign of what, he still wasn't sure.

"How are you?" he asked, then rolled his eyes. That's what he came up with after all those miles, all this time? Small talk for the win.

"I'm fine. Busy, of course. I've been working a lot."

She didn't say "miserable without you," or "sobbing into my coffee cup every morning." Maybe coming up here had been a mistake. "That's good."

She stopped walking and stared at him. "No, it's not."

"You're right, it's not." It meant she was still the same woman who had bailed on him and Ellie to work over and over again. The same woman who had escaped into emails and phone calls when she didn't want to face her fears. "I was just being polite."

"I should have more of a life. I should have hours in my day where I hang out with my girlfriends or go on a date or just go shopping. Instead, I have this office." She waved at the behemoth of a building behind them. "And I decided, well, cemented my decision after the meeting I just had, that... I don't want to go home to an empty house anymore."

Go on a date. Empty house. Sounded like she wanted to move on. Except she was holding his hand

and looking into his eyes, and he was still trying to figure out what the hell was going on.

"What are you saying, Vivian? Because I didn't come here to hear that you want to date someone else."

A smile he couldn't read curved across her face. "Just walk with me, a little longer. Please?"

A slight breeze kicked up and rattled through the trees. The rest of the world was quiet, the traffic behind this woods-lined path almost nonexistent.

The sun had begun its descent, oranges and mauves washing over the world. A bit of bright orange light peeked through the trees for a moment, then disappeared. They rounded a bend, and the path curved farther into the woods.

"I walk this path almost every day," she said. "Or at least, I do now. I've tried to get out in the sunshine and air more often since I came back to Durham. Sometimes I walk alone, sometimes I take Ellie with me, in that stroller I bought her that cost a mint, and I had to have redelivered here." She laughed. "Anyway, I like this path because it reminds me of Stone Gap."

It did have that leafy green, quiet peace about it that Nick had found in Stone Gap. Almost as if they'd discovered an unsung corner of the world. Did she miss the town? Or him? "It's a lot like the road that runs beside the lake. Except for the lack of a lake."

"It also has one other thing that we had in Stone Gap." They turned again, and from here the path spilled into a park. A playground sat to the left, built on a rubber surface designed to be soft when little ones slipped and fell. A small pond lay in the far distance, a dock jutting to the center. A heron picked his way among the grassy shore. But it was the circular building on the right that drew Nick's eye.

A gazebo. Like the one in Stone Gap, this one had been decorated for the holidays. Similar white lights were twined among the railings and rafters, and giant red bows hung on each of the side panels. As they approached, the lights blinked on, glowing softly in the gathering dusk.

"I come here every night at this time. I never even knew the gazebo existed until I started walking the path. But then I found this and…well, some nights it's hard to leave it and go home."

"Why?" He prayed she'd say what he wanted to hear, that she came to remember the night they shared—that it meant as much to her as it did to him.

"Because it reminds me of our gazebo," she said.

The words *our gazebo* made that hope spring to life in his chest again. "Vivian—"

"But then I realize nothing has changed. I'm still here, you're still there." She drew in a breath and raised her chin. "And even though I told you it was over… I kind of hoped you'd reach out anyway."

Yeah, there was that. Every day that passed, he'd wanted to call, but he'd either caved to fear or stubbornness or some kind of convoluted male pride. "It's not like I haven't thought about contacting you. I have. A thousand times. It wasn't until I screwed up a French omelet that I realized I was avoiding talking to you because I was afraid." He shook his head. He had driven all the way up here, maybe because he was feeling sentimental, maybe because he was a fool, but if he didn't say what he'd come here to say, he knew he'd regret it the rest of his life. "I don't want to end up like my father, letting the words go unsaid for years. So here I am, and I'm going to say them." He took a deep breath. "I love you, Vivian. I want to be with you. I should have gone after you when you left two weeks ago, but I was afraid."

"Afraid that I'd say no again?"

"You did kinda run out the door when I said I wanted forever." But so far, she was still here. Still looking at him with those big blue eyes and still holding his hand.

Her laughter was merry and light. "I did. You scared me, too, Nick. I was afraid to have the one thing that I had convinced myself I could live without. A family." She led him up the gazebo steps and into the magic spot in the center where the lights above formed a halo on the floor. She shifted into his arms. She felt good there, really good. "All my life, I've focused on being smart, strong, successful. That turned into pouring everything I had into my career. That was my safety net. If I could keep succeeding there... It's just like when I was a little girl and thought if only I was smart enough or neat enough or polite enough, my mother would step up, stop drinking and be a real mom. Instead, I was so busy being perfect and successful that I forgot to connect with the people I love. To build relationships. I was the one who wasn't taking risks with other people. People like you. And yet, you know what? My sister still loved me and thought I would be a better mother than her."

"Maybe she saw something in you that you didn't see. Like I do." Damn, Vivian was beautiful and smart. The day she'd walked into his life had made him one of the luckiest men on earth. It had just taken him a while to realize that.

"Maybe," Vivian said. "But Sammie is also far smarter than I give her credit for. She asked for help when she was overwhelmed. Granted, running away and leaving Ellie in the kitchen unsupervised wasn't the best way to do that, but she wasn't afraid to admit she couldn't be a mom on her own. Since we got back here, she's been living with me. And I've been taking Ellie to work for the couple hours a day when my schedule overlaps Sammie's at the diner."

"Really? That's great." That explained the ease with Ellie, the conversation about bottles and teething. Vivian had changed, in a lot of good ways, since that day in the kitchen of the inn.

"And in doing that, I realized I could do all those things I had been afraid of before. Raise a child. Fall in love. Create a home. Have a merry Christmas."

He thought of his grandmother's house. The tree still sat in the living room, with only the lights on the branches. Since Vivian left, he hadn't been able to bring himself to finish the decorating or to turn the lights on again. Nothing in that house felt right, not without her. "Wait. Did you just say fall in love?"

She nodded, her smile wide and unmistakable. "I fell in love with you, Nick, the night we had that date in the gazebo. It was because of how considerate you were. With the heater, the lights for Ellie in the tree. I just took a while to admit it to myself. And to you."

"That's okay. It took me a while to come after you and tell you that you are the best thing that's ever happened to me." He brushed away an errant tendril of her hair. "I want to spend Christmas with you, Vivian. This Christmas and next Christmas and all the ones after that."

She shook her head. "We can't do that here."

His heart dropped. Damn it. Had he wasted all this time? Misunderstood what she just said?

"I won't be here for Christmas, because…" Vivian said, "I want Ellie's first Christmas to be special, even if she is very unlikely to remember it. And I wanted to give Sammie a real holiday too. So I took a week off, and called the inn. Except there's one problem."

"The inn is closed for Christmas." A smile began to tease at the edges of his mouth.

"Yep. So I'm going to need another place to stay. You see, I really want Ellie's first Christmas to be in Stone Gap. And sadly, there's no other B and B in town. I do hear, however, that there is a mostly empty house that already has a very special lopsided tree."

The smile spread across his face and felt like it reached all the way to his toes. "That house also has a nursery already set up." He couldn't bring himself to walk in that room since they left, never mind bring the crib back to Mavis.

The tease he loved lit her eyes. "Are you accepting reservations? Otherwise, my plan was to just show up on your doorstep, sort of like a baby showing up on your kitchen table."

Damn, she felt good in his arms. He never wanted to let go of her again. "I'm sorry, but you have to be a part of the family to stay at 32 Lakeshore Drive."

She raised her gaze to his. "And am I? Part of the family?"

"Honey, you are all the family I want." He leaned down and kissed her then, slow and sweet and tender. She raised on her toes and wrapped her arms around his neck, and when Vivian kissed him back, Nick's heart soared. They stayed there, until the sun went down and the air chilled, and then they went home.

The next morning, Vivian woke up in Nick's arms. The sun had yet to rise, but she couldn't wait. All her life, she'd dreamed of this moment, this exact kind of day, and now she had it, with her sister sleeping in the next room and Ellie in the crib across the hall. And the man she loved right beside her, still tangled up with her. "It's Christmas, Nick," she whispered. "Wake up so we can go downstairs and open presents."

He opened his eyes and gave her a smile. "I already opened mine."

She laughed. "That was last night. Today, I want a Christmas to remember. For all of us."

For the first time in his life, Nick Jackson was up at dawn on Christmas morning. There were no servants to make breakfast or butlers to hand out the presents. There was just them, in the house that held all of Nick's best memories.

They went downstairs, still in their pajamas, followed a moment later by Sammie and Ellie, and the four of them sat around that lopsided tree, with its lights and the dozens of decorations they'd hung together the night before. Later, there would be pancakes and presents, but in that moment, watching the rainbow of lights dance across the features of the woman he loved, Nick realized even Santa couldn't top this gift.

* * * * *

Don't miss Grant's story,
the next installment in
New York Times *bestselling author Shirley Jump's*
The Stone Gap Inn miniseries
Coming soon to Harlequin Special Edition.

SPECIAL EXCERPT FROM

H HARLEQUIN®

SPECIAL EDITION

Despite lying on her résumé, Amanda Lowery still manages to land a job designing Halcyon House for Blake Randall—and a place to stay over Christmas. Neither of them have had much to celebrate, but with Blake's grieving nephew staying at Halcyon, too, they're all hoping for some Christmas magic.

Read on for a sneak preview of Jo McNally's It Started at Christmas…, *a prequel in the Gallant Lake Stories miniseries.*

"Amanda, I didn't mean to upset you. I don't ever want to do anything that scares you."

She sucked in a deep, ragged breath, looking so terribly lost and sad. Her eyelids fluttered open. She stared straight ahead, talking to his chest.

"You don't understand, Blake. There are days when… when everything scares me." Her voice was barely above a whisper. His heart jumped. He thought of that first day, when she ended up unconscious in his arms.

Everything scares me.

She'd kicked her shoes off earlier, and in her bare feet the top of her head barely reached his shoulders. He put his fingers under her chin and gently tipped her head back.

He wanted to kiss this woman.

Wait. What?

No. That would be wild. He couldn't kiss her. Shouldn't. But how could he not?

Her hair tumbled off her shoulders and down her back in golden curls. Before he knew it, his free hand was slowly twisting into those curls. She didn't pull away. Didn't look away. He lowered his head until his face was just above hers. He felt her breath on his skin. She smelled like citrus and spice and blueberries and red wine. Her lips parted and she stared at him with her enormous eyes.

"I swear I don't want to scare you, Amanda. But… may I kiss you?" His voice was a raw whisper. "Please let me kiss you."

His words came out as a plea. He'd never begged for anything before in his life. But here he was, begging this sweet woman for a kiss. Ready to drop to his knees if that was what it took. He heard his father's voice in his head, mocking his weakness. That was when he started to straighten, started to come to his senses. Then he heard her whispered answer.

"Yes."

Was there any sweeter word in the world? Adrenaline surged through his body, and his hand tightened in her hair. His eyes opened to meet those two oceans of blue. Dangerous blue. Deep enough to drown in.

She was frightened, but she was trusting him. And that realization scared him to death.

Don't miss It Started at Christmas… *by Jo McNally, available December 2019 wherever Harlequin® Special Edition books and ebooks are sold.*

Harlequin.com

Don't miss *Stealing Kisses in the Snow*,
the heart-tugging romance in

JO McNALLY's

Rendezvous Falls series centered around
a matchmaking book club in
Rendezvous Falls, New York.

As Christmas draws ever closer, so do Piper and
Logan. Could these two opposites discover that all
they want this Christmas is each other?

Order your copy today!

Looking for more satisfying love stories
with community and family at their core?

Check out **Harlequin® Special Edition**
and **Love Inspired®** books!

New books available every month!

CONNECT WITH US AT:

Facebook.com/groups/HarlequinConnection

 Facebook.com/HarlequinBooks

Twitter.com/HarlequinBooks

Instagram.com/HarlequinBooks

Pinterest.com/HarlequinBooks

ReaderService.com

**ROMANCE WHEN
YOU NEED IT**

HFGENRE2018

Looking for inspiration in tales
of hope, faith and heartfelt romance?

Check out **Love Inspired®** and
Love Inspired® Suspense books!

New books available every month!

CONNECT WITH US AT:

Facebook.com/groups/HarlequinConnection

 Facebook.com/HarlequinBooks

 Twitter.com/HarlequinBooks

 Instagram.com/HarlequinBooks

Pinterest.com/HarlequinBooks

ReaderService.com

Love Inspired®

Love Harlequin romance?

DISCOVER.

Be the first to find out about promotions, news and exclusive content!

Facebook.com/HarlequinBooks

Twitter.com/HarlequinBooks

Instagram.com/HarlequinBooks

Pinterest.com/HarlequinBooks

ReaderService.com

EXPLORE.

Sign up for the Harlequin e-newsletter and download a free book from any series at **TryHarlequin.com.**

CONNECT.

Join our Harlequin community to share your thoughts and connect with other romance readers!
Facebook.com/groups/HarlequinConnection

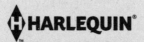

**ROMANCE WHEN
YOU NEED IT**